THE RENEGADE

THE RENEGADE

Cliff Farrell

LP
W
F 245 re
JV

Thorndike Press
Waterville, Maine USA

Chivers Press
Bath, England

This Large Print edition is published by Thorndike Press®, USA and by Chivers Press, England.

Published in 2003 in the U.S. by arrangement with Golden West Literary Agency.

Published in 2003 in the U.K. by arrangement with Golden West.

U.S. Hardcover 0-7862-5472-6 (Western Series)
U.K. Hardcover 0-7540-7283-5 (Chivers Large Print)
U.K. Softcover 0-7540-7284-3 (Camden Large Print)

The text of this Large Print edition is unabridged.
Other aspects of the book may vary from the original edition.

Set in 16 pt. Plantin by Christina S. Huff.

Printed in the United States on permanent paper.

British Library Cataloguing-in-Publication Data available

Library of Congress Cataloging-in-Publication Data

Farrell, Cliff.
    The renegade / Cliff Farrell.
        p. cm.
    ISBN 0-7862-5472-6 (lg. print : hc : alk. paper)
    1. Large type books.   I. Title.
PS3556.A766R46 2003
    813'.54—dc21   2003045262

THE RENEGADE

FOREWORD

As the Founder/CEO of NAVH, the only national health agency solely devoted to those who, although not totally blind, have an eye disease which could lead to serious visual impairment, I am pleased to recognize Thorndike Press as one of the leading publishers in the large print field.

Founded in 1954 in San Francisco to prepare large print textbooks for partially seeing children, NAVH became the pioneer and standard setting agency in the preparation of large type.

Today, those publishers who meet our standards carry the prestigious "Seal of Approval" indicating high quality large print. We are delighted that Thorndike Press is one of the publishers whose titles meet these standards. We are also pleased to recognize the significant contribution Thorndike Press is making in this important and growing field.

Lorraine H. Marchi, L.H.D.
Founder/CEO
NAVH

Chapter 1

Mike McVey spent the biggest part of a week getting the gold across the Missouri River. It was a tough, dangerous job that he handled very cautiously. For once in his life, he was forcing himself to watch every step, and not charge in, regardless of consequences. He didn't aim to lose his scalp now, after spending months panning the dust out of the stream he had stumbled on in Sioux country the previous fall.

It was now April, and the ice had gone out of the river only a week or so before he arrived on the west bank with his fortune. The river was beginning to rise, but the ford, which was nearly half a mile wide, was still shallow, with only a few spots of swimming water between the islands and rock chains.

It wasn't the river that had him weighing every move before he chanced it. There were marks of travois poles and pony hoofs at the ford, but these were at least a day old. They didn't exactly worry him, for the moccasin tracks that accompanied the travois were those of squaws. There had been two women, perhaps three with the travois.

It wasn't legal for Indians to cross from treaty country to the east side under present conditions without approval from the commander at Fort Flagg, but violations were winked at in the cases of small parties for the sake of store owners at the settlement near the fort who picked up profit by trading with the visitors, as long as the trade wasn't in guns, knives or ammunition.

Still, an occasional lone traveler on the east side vanished at times, or an outlying settler's cabin would be hit, and no one left to name the guilty. These usually brought stern warnings from the Army to the Sioux or Cheyenne that such outrages must be stopped and the guilty parties punished. That was as far as it usually went. Neither side crossed the river in force, particularly the Army, which was not anxious to touch off the big plains war that everyone felt was brewing.

McVey had built a crude raft of driftwood, not big enough to float both himself and the two pokes of dust which was all he would trust to the river on each crossing. He made the trips only at first daybreak or at deep dusk, pushing the raft ahead of him, wading mainly and swimming the few stretches of deeper water. On the east shore he'd cache the pokes and hide out until he deemed it safe to make the return for more gold.

He was in no hurry. No hurry at all. He estimated that he had about sixty thousand dollars worth of the grainy dust in the pokes he'd made of elk and buffalo hide. That was enough to keep him on easy street if he treated it right. In the past, he had liked to play poker and enjoy life, but he didn't intend to gamble with this stake in high-limit games or take wild fliers in other directions. He had already done just these things. He had bet his life every day, and sometimes every minute, during those months. Now he was almost in the clear.

Emboldened, he made his last trip in broad day, at noon. Abandoning the raft, he swam his roan saddle horse and the two pack ponies across. He was out of treaty country, at least. Not that he was entirely out of danger. Lone scalp hunters and small raiding parties still crossed the river. But, within reach was Fort Flagg and stagecoach or steamboat transportation. Also, not far away would be the farm of Esau Solomon where he would find a friend, a roof to sleep under and someone to talk to.

He kept assuring himself he had earned what he had won. A winter of wresting it from that harsh land, alone, regardless of the Indian hazard, made a man feel that it was really his. Still, there was that blasted voice of conscience that kept jeering and nagging, and wouldn't be quiet. It kept telling him he was going against the principles for which he had stood. It was always reminding him that, when you looked at it from the Indian's viewpoint, the gold didn't belong to him, but to the tribes.

He promised himself one thing. He would never tell where he had made the strike. He had panned the gold from deep in the hunting grounds of the tribes which was pledged to them forever by treaty. When the treaty had been agreed, the white men did not know there was gold in the Black Hills. They still didn't know.

Only Mike McVey knew for sure, and he also knew what would happen if the secret got out. It had happened in other places when the stampedes started. The Indians would lose their hunting grounds, and a lot of them would lose their lives, and others their way of existence.

It wasn't that he owed anything to the Indians, or that he carried a banner in their behalf, although some of the staff at Fort Flagg, Colonel Roscoe Cool in particular, had other opinions. It was that, disastrously for his Army career, he had seen the thing from the Indian viewpoint as well as that of the Army. He also believed that any man, any army, or any government, should keep its word. A treaty was a word of honor in his opinion.

He knew he was debating it with himself with a forked tongue. He had broken the treaty himself, gone against his principles, the day he had dipped his skillet into the sand along a creek in the Black Hills where he had seen the dull shine of yellow. He had known from first glimpse that it was the real thing. He had been immediately cast under its spell.

He was on his way to Cheyenne at the time, for personal reasons. That was after Colonel Cool had suggested that he no longer needed a brash first lieutenant who didn't look at things the way his commanding officer did.

He could have taken steamboat to Council Bluff, and the Union Pacific to Cheyenne, but that cost money, a commodity not too plentiful at any time with him. In addition, he already possessed a good saddle horse and two pack ponies that had been his personal property for hunting trips. The shortest way to Cheyenne, for a horseman, was across three hundred miles of Indian country — hostile country. Even though he had a reputation as a friend of the tribes, he had held no illusions as to what would have happened to him if he had been caught by the tribesmen.

He'd spent the autumn and winter on the placer, panning two miles of the stream before pulling out. It had been harsh, agonizing labor, often in freezing water during lulls in winter's storms. He had worked warily, trying to make sure he was leaving no sign of each day's panning to attract the eye of a passing Indian hunter. He had lived like a beaver in a brushy covert a considerable distance from the stream. There had been days at a time when blizzards had kept him prisoner in his hideout. Then the chinooks would come and he'd frenziedly work the stream again.

He had ranged far for game and other food. Several times he had missed discovery by the thinnest of margins. On many occasions he had lain, rifle cocked for hours, waiting for them to come.

They had not come for him. Now he was across the Missouri with the gold. It was human avarice, of course, that had driven him. He admitted that, not being a man to make excuses for his failings.

He could have been taken for an Indian at

first glance. He wore misshapen breeches of elkhide that had been cut by himself with a skinning knife and bound by animal sinew for thread. He wore a tattered hunting shirt of the same construction, and moccasins to match. He had long since abandoned the cavalry hat with which he had set out westward, and now had a strip of elkhide around his forehead to keep his long, dark hair out of his eyes. He still had his razor and shaving soap, but hadn't had a chance to use them for a week, and a stiff stubble of black beard covered his lean jaws. He was twenty pounds lighter than the previous fall, and he had always been a sort of a beanpole, six feet two, with no meat to spare on his frame.

Yes, he figured he'd paid the price for what he was bringing out of treaty country. The heaviest toll had been exacted by loneliness. Except for two visits to a trading post far up the Missouri to buy flour and other necessities, paying with fox, beaver and wolf pelts, he had not seen another human to talk to.

And Mike McVey was a gregarious man who liked to put his foot on a barroom rail, flick his hat to the back of his head, and pass time with friends. He was twenty-eight years old, but right now he felt as ancient as the land around him. He made friends easily and they stood by him. It was the same the other way. Colonel Cool, for instance. Ironjaw, the men called him. He and Mike had crossed swords, in a manner of speaking, on several occasions. The colonel would like nothing better than to slap him into a cell and throw away the key. Possession of the gold would be prime evidence that it had come from treaty country. The fact that traders and whisky peddlers violated the treaty with impunity was ignored, but it would not be ignored in Mike's case if the colonel had anything to do with it.

When he emerged on the east shore with his horses after the final trip he drew a long, full breath into his lungs. He laughed. The sound startled him. It sounded like the rusty hinge on a gate that had not been opened for a long time. He could not believe it had been his own mouth from which it had come, and he looked around, ready to dive to cover. After a moment he attempted it again, just for a test.

"Gawdamighty!" he told the horses. "It's high time I come back to the human race."

Why, blast it, he used to sing a lusty baritone in the officers' quartet at the fort. Maybe his brain had turned to tin, like the sound of his voice. He'd seen others who came out of the plains with cracked voices,

14

cracked grins — and cracked brains. They were wanderers who had lost some of their mental buttons from being alone too long. A man could go down the wrong path just by talking in whispers to whisky jays and prairie jays for months at a time, as he had done. And there had been no laughing nor talking out loud at all. A voice carried far in the silence of the wilds.

The country west of the river had been full of Indian sign. He had crossed the trails of big villages on the move, and of sizable hunting parties scouring the plains for game. All of the villages seemed to have been heading toward the Missouri.

However, except for the tracks of the travois party, there was no evidence that any other travelers had used the ford in some time. Wet and shivering, he built a fire and remained with it until the numbness had faded from his fibers and his clothing and gear were dried.

He loaded the gold on the packsaddles of the ponies, and saddled the roan, which, like himself, was honed to sinew and whipcord. Sundown was near when he doused the fire and rode away, leading the ponies. Esau Solomon's place could not be more than half a dozen miles away, although he was still uncertain of his location.

The horses moved along briskly as though they, too, sensed that the worst was over. He followed the course of the river where exposed sandbars and clay cutbanks began to gleam as white as bones against the blackness of the water as the day faded.

Twilight had come when he began seeing familiar-looking knolls and bluffs on the skyline. He peered eagerly, sure that Esau's place would be showing up soon — provided he hadn't changed location. That was unlikely, for Esau Solomon was a man of the earth, bound to it by love of the soil. Born into slavery, he had drifted, emancipated, to the frontier after the Civil War, and had married a comely Cheyenne girl, daughter of a chief, and had settled down on a promising plot of land on the east side of the river where he grew corn, potatoes, squash, and other vegetables, hunted, trapped, and chopped driftwood to length for sale to the steamboat boiler rooms in order to raise cash.

The roan was the first to scent the chimney smoke. Its ears came to a point. Mike laughed, and now the sound was better. Emerging from the brush, he saw Esau's cleared land ahead. Tattered mounds of crumpled cornshocks that had survived the winter rustled in the slow draw of air

16

from the river. Esau's garden patch had been readied for crops that would be planted when the threat of frost was over. It stood back of a riprap barrier of driftwood, brush and rocks that Esau had built in his endless battle against jackrabbits and deer.

A window light showed beyond the field. Smoke drifted from the rock chimney of Esau's cabin which was flanked by a pole corral and a smokehouse and shed. Mike rode closer, circling the fenced vegetable field, then suddenly pulled the horses to a stop.

An Indian lodge was pitched near Esau's cabin. Mike studied it and saw that it was a small lodge of the kind that were carried on hunting trips or for visits. Esau had guests, and the chances were they were relatives of his Cheyenne wife. That, at least, would explain the travois marks at the river ford.

Disappointed, he sat debating it in his mind. Esau, he could trust with the secret of the gold, even with his life. In fact Esau had once saved his life. But strangers — and Cheyennes from treaty country in particular . . .

The roan and the ponies began to stir uneasily and wanted to turn away. He became aware that eerie sounds came from the cabin. At this distance they were so faint he barely could make them out, but the horses were hearing them plainly and did not like what they heard. Finally he realized that what he was hearing was the singsong chant of Indian women offering a prayer to the Great Spirit.

He looked around. Nearby was a gully, along whose flank brush grew thickly. It had been formed by storm runoff in the past and led to the river a few hundred yards farther on, but it was dry now. He located a crevice just below its rim in which he cached the pokes of gold. He covered the cache with dry brush and brushed out his moccasin tracks as best he could in the moonlight. The whole operation took only a few minutes. The hiding place was not the safest in the world, but he expected to be back shortly.

He mounted and prodded the uneasy horses across the flat toward the cabin and dismounted. The door was closed, but the curtain had not been drawn at the window from which came the lamplight. He peered through the glass.

Three Indian women squatted near a pallet on which lay Esau's young wife. Her Cheyenne name meant Dawn-in-the-Sky. One of the three squaws was her mother, Elk Woman, who was the wife of the important chief, Gray Buffalo. Mike had met her in the past during visits to Esau's home. Elk Woman was rocking back and forth on her knees and sounding a sad lamentation. A withered Indian woman, whom Mike guessed was the grandmother, also was mumbling the chant. Dawn-in-the-Sky's sister, who was a year or so younger, bent over the pallet, moving a turkey feather fan. Mike saw that the patient was burning with fever.

There was no sign of Esau. Mike moved to the door and knocked. "I'm Mike McVey," he called. "You remember me, Elk Woman. I'm Esau's friend and a friend of Dawn-in-the-Sky."

Elk Woman remembered. The chanting broke off. Moccasins shuffled on the packed clay floor and the door opened. Elk Woman stood before him, covering her face with her hands, for it is not seemly for a woman to show such grief before the eyes of an outsider.

"What is it, Mother?" Mike asked.

The Cheyenne woman was unable to answer. When Mike started to enter she tried to stand in his way, but he pushed past and bent over the Indian girl on the pallet. Dawn-in-the-Sky recognized him. She looked up at him with both anguish and sudden wild hope in dark pools of eyes that were afire with her travail.

"What is it, honey?" Mike asked huskily. "You're sick."

"Very, very sick, McVey," she murmured. She had learned English at a missionary school. "The baby, it will not be born. I am on fire and I think the gates of hell are open for me. I do not want to die. We have been so happy here, me and my Esau."

"Don't talk like that," Mike said. "You're not going to die. Where's Esau?"

"He went to the fort to bring the yellowleg doctor to help me and the baby."

"To Flagg? When did he go?"

Dawn-in-the-Sky tried to remember, but her fevered mind would not sustain the thought. Mike turned to her mother. Elk Woman understood English and could speak it too, but she refused to use the tongue of people she considered her enemy. She used the sign language and a few words of Cheyenne that she knew Mike would understand. She indicated the rising of the sun, then its setting and drew finger pictures of Esau riding away on an animal with pointed ears. Esau had owned a mule that he used both with the plow and as a saddle animal.

"He rode to the fort before sunrise today?" Mike exclaimed.

Elk Woman nodded. No, she had no word from Esau since he had left. Mike was puzzled. Fort Flagg was only ten miles or less away. Esau should have been back many hours ago.

— He bent over Dawn-in-the-Sky. Esau had given her the name of Ruth, taken from the Bible. The Book itself lay open on a table nearby. Mike had given it to the big black man as a Christmas present in the past. Esau had laboriously taught himself to read the messages that had become the guide-points of his life.

Mike could see that Dawn-in-the-Sky had told the truth. She was near death. There was nothing he could do for her. Elk Woman and the grandmother were experienced at this sort of thing, and it was evident they had been working to the best of their knowledge to bring the baby into the world. They had failed. A trained surgeon was needed, if the Cheyenne girl was to live.

"I'll fetch the yellowleg doctor, Ruth," he said. "I'll find Esau."

"Esau is dead," she said. "If he lived he would have come back to me. Nothing would have stopped him but death." She added, "He is my husband."

She spoke the word with vast pride and tenderness. Mike feared that again she

21

might be speaking the truth. He knew how unbreakable was the bond between the black man and the Cheyenne girl.

He left the cabin and ran to the roan horse. "Take care of the ponies, Mother," he called to Elk Woman who stood in the cabin door. Mounting, he prodded the roan into a gallop. Then he pulled the horse to a stop after it had made only a few strides.

He was listening to a new, alien sound in the night. It was a low, throbbing beat that grew louder. It was the mechanical voice of a steam engine driving the paddle-wheel of a river boat. The Army owned and leased packets to supply the posts along the upper Missouri.

Mike had a new thought. He rode the roan to the cutbank overlooking the river. Leaping down and pulling his rifle from the boot, he scrambled down the bank and waded and leaped across shallows until he stood near the deeper channel of the main stream. The running lights of a steamboat were appearing around a bend upstream, bearing down on his position. He guessed that the craft was returning from forts far up river and heading for nearby Fort Flagg.

The pilot was following the deeper channel which apparently ran so close to where he stood that a landing should be easy for the flat-bottomed craft, built to float "on a heavy dew" as the saying went on the river.

Mike fired three shots into the air — the customary distress signal. He heard a bell clang in the engineroom. A voice bawled an order from the top deck of the craft. The paddles slowed.

"Who in Tophet air yuh?" a deep voice boomed through a megaphone.

Mike recognized that voice. That also identified the packet as the *Far Frontier*, which was leased to the Army for supply and troop transport. Its skipper was a beefy, tough Irishman named Pat Flannery. He and Mike had struck sparks whenever they had met. It was Flannery's boast that he could lick any man on the river and he was always willing to prove it.

"This is Mike McVey," Mike shouted. "Lay to and drop your plank here. There's deep water right up to the gravel."

He heard Flannery's snort of disdain. "Ah, Mike McVey, is it now?" the steamboat captain replied. "Alive an' givin' orders to his betters. Could ye not stay dead? Colonel Cool posted you as gone to your just deserts months ago. By what impudence do you delay a packet bound on important Army business?"

"We've got a sick girl here," Mike

shouted. "She needs a doctor and in a hurry. I was starting to ride to the fort to fetch the post surgeon, but it will save time to take her aboard."

"A sick girl? An' who is it?"

"Esau Solomon's wife," Mike replied. "The baby wants to be born but there's bad trouble."

"What?" Flannery bellowed. "Do you mean you're flaggin' me down on account of an Injun an' a nigger squawman?"

"On account of a girl who needs a doctor in a hurry!" Mike roared back. "Swing that tub in here. I'll need help to carry her aboard. If you've got a stretcher handy that will be welcome."

"You've got a brass nerve delayin' this packet, even if you're tellin' the truth, which I doubt," Flannery replied. "Do ye think I'd risk me pilot an' captain's license by maybe snaggin' this steamboat on account of a squaw? Chances are it's an ambush anyway. How do I know there ain't a Sioux war party bushed up, waitin' 'til you bait me in reach? I always figgered you was more Injun that white, McVey. Next time I run acrost you I'll beat the tar out'n you for tryin' to make a fool out o' me."

The engineroom bell clanged again. The paddlewheel took a heavier bite in the water.

24

The *Far Frontier* began to forge ahead downstream.

Mike lifted the rifle and fired. The bullet kicked up water a dozen feet ahead of the boat's prow. "Heave to!" he shouted. "Flannery, you fool, I'm telling you the truth. Ruth Solomon is a human being. Bring that packet around, blast you."

Flannery's reply was a string of profanity. Mike levered a shell into the chamber and fired again. He heard glass shatter in the pilothouse window. He had aimed high, not wanting to injure anyone.

"I'll beat you within an inch of your life if you don't bring that boat around, Flannery!" he yelled.

The *Far Frontier* kept going. Flannery's renewed screeches of rage faded downstream.

Chapter 2

Seething with anger and frustration, Mike ran to the roan and mounted. He pushed the horse to its limit over the rough, wheel-track trail. The route by land was considerably shorter than the course of the river which meandered west in a wide loop at this point. He occasionally sighted the running lights of the *Far Frontier* some distance across the flats and falling well back of him.

The window lights of the straggling civilian settlement that was named Flagg City appeared and hung tantalizingly in the night for a long time before he drew close enough to make out the shape of the buildings and the bulk of the military stockade which stood on higher ground. The fort should have been asleep at this hour after taps, but its wide log gate was open and there was great activity inside the stockade, and particularly at the landing below the bluff.

Floating docks, pontooned on barrels, lay against the shore. A packet, bearing the name *Far West*, which was a sister ship to

Flannery's *Far Frontier*, was swinging in for a landing, arriving from downstream.

Mike stood in the stirrups, peering, as he rode nearer. The fort's brass band, in parade dress, was drawn up near the landing, its leader poising the baton for the proper moment to strike up. The men of the two companies of the regiment that garrisoned the fort were drawn up at rigid attention on foot above the landing. The officers, in parade dress with swords and sashes, were assembled in a double file on the floating dock. Colonel Cool, immaculate and rigidly military, stood between the columns of his subordinates, waiting. The wives of the officers stood in the background, garbed in their flowery best.

Torches burned on the landing and on the parapet of the fort. Basket flares blazed on the steamboat as it edged toward the dock, the paddlewheel slowed to steerageway. A group of ladies stood on the deck of the packet.

Two were young, comely girls, fashionably garbed in white and pink, with small bonnets perched on carefully done hair. One was a brunette, the other had coppery-gold hair glinting in the torchlight. With them were two older women, stylishly and expensively dressed.

Standing in attendance with the arriving ladies, in dress uniform, was the man Mike had come to find — Marshall Prine, the post surgeon.

Colonel Cool raised a hand, and cannon blasted a salute from the fort. The unexpected reports sent Mike's lathered mount into a frenzy of pitching. Taken by surprise, he found himself flying through the air. He landed flat on his back with a jolt that left him breathless.

He staggered to his feet, gasping. His downfall had taken place in the background and was being ignored by nearly everyone except the coppery-haired girl on the packet. She was shaking with laughter, holding her hands to her face to conceal her mirth.

Mike glared, trying to regain his dignity, and to freeze her out of her amusement. That only increased her choked laughter. He stalked to where the roan had halted, seized up the dragging reins and tethered the animal to a stump.

The band struck up. The tune was "The Girl I Left Behind Me." Kerchiefs of the officers' ladies began fluttering — also on command from Colonel Roscoe Cool. Stevedores leaped to moor the packet. The gangplank descended on the dock. An officer uttered a crisp order. Swords were drawn and swung aloft to form a shimmering steel arch. Colonel Cool marched up the plank to meet the ladies.

Mike moved in and took a position at the shore end of the dock. The colonel had acknowledged Marsh Prine's salute, and was being introduced to the ladies. Then he offered his arms and headed for the dock, escorting the two younger visitors. Prine followed with the two older ladies.

Mike intercepted Prine as he emerged from beneath the arch of swords. "I want to speak to you for a moment, Marsh," he said. "It's urgent."

Prine peered for seconds before recognizing him. He was a competent and efficient medical officer, having graduated from one of the best schools in the East. He was from an aristocratic family and never let himself forget it.

He tried to move on ahead, his hands on the arms of the two girls, ignoring Mike.

"Marsh!" Mike spoke again. "It's desperate. A girl is dying. She needs a doctor. Now!"

Colonel Cool, a few paces ahead, halted. The whole procession came to a stop. "What's this?" Cool barked. "Is that really you, McVey? So you're still alive? What have you turned into, a whisky runner, a squaw-man? Are you drunk? What do you mean by trying to make a scene at a time like this?"

Mike had resigned his commission as an officer under Cool after a series of clashes with his superior over Cool's early zeal for killing Indians.

That old feud was in the colonel's bleak eyes now. "Speak, man, or do you want to be thrown into a cell?" he barked.

"A young girl is dying," Mike said. "A baby is being born and she needs a doctor as soon as possible. I came to find Dr. Prine."

He had the futile feeling of having gone through this before, and expected the frustration to be repeated. But he had to keep trying — for Esau's sake — for Dawn-in-the-Sky's sake.

"It's Esau Solomon's wife," he added.

"You can't be serious!" the colonel exploded. "Do you think Dr. Prine can go running to help every squaw that bears a baby, and a black one at that, in this case? I know this man who call himself Esau Solomon."

"Ruth Solomon is the daughter of Gray Buffalo," Mike said. "She's no ordinary squaw — not that this matters. She needs help."

"But, man, don't you realize that tonight is one of the happiest moments in Dr.

Prine's life? He's to be married in a day or two and his fiancée has just arrived after a long journey."

So that was what all the finery and music and bowing and scraping was about. "But, it's only little more than an hour's ride to Esau's place," Mike argued desperately. "Dr. Prine could probably be back soon."

Prine spoke. "McVey you *must* be drunk — or crazy. Any squaw could take care of a thing like that. You know that."

"She's got her mother and other Cheyenne women," Mike said. "But she needs expert help."

Prine turned his back and addressed the colonel. "I went through this a few hours ago with the black squawman, sir," he said. "I explained to him as reasonably as I could that it's impossible. He got ugly. Tried to tell me I had to come with him. Had to, mind you. I was forced to order him —"

"You've seen Esau Solomon?" Mike broke in. "Where?"

Prine continued to ignore him. "There's nothing I can do, my dears," he said to the young ladies. "You understand that things are different out here on the frontier."

The coppery-haired girl spoke. "Oh, Marsh, couldn't you at least try? This man says it won't take long."

31

The dark-haired girl put in a word also. "Maybe you should go, Marsh. We'd all feel better about it. Isn't this what started the trouble with the colored man down the river?"

Colonel Cool spoke. "It's impossible, ladies. I forbid it. The officers and their wives have gone to great trouble and expense to honor you. We can't insult them by having the prospective bridegroom off on some wild goose chase on the word of this renegade. There's likely no real need for the doctor. A banquet and a dance has been arranged. I won't allow the evening to be spoiled."

The colonel started moving ahead again, almost forcibly taking the two girls with him. Prine followed with the older women. Mike moved again into his path intending to plead with him, but the colonel barked an order. "Sergeant, see to it that this man doesn't further annoy any officer or guest of the post. If he causes any more trouble lock him in the guardhouse until he sobers up."

A sergeant and three men from the ranks surrounded Mike and crowded him off the landing. The colonel led the guests up the path to the stockade gate, the officers and their wives following. The band struck up and led the cavalry companies into the parade ground inside the stockade.

"You all right, Lieutenant Mc— I mean Mr. McVey?" the sergeant asked. He was a man who had soldiered in Mike's command in the past.

"I'm all right, Smitty," Mike said. "You and the men get along. You'll be missing a drink or two."

He was left alone on the shore. He turned. Two stevedores were carrying a limp weight between them across the gangplank to the dock. They swung their burden for a moment, then released it so that it landed heavily on the shore barely clear of the floating dock and almost in the margin of the river.

The weight they had jettisoned was the body of Esau Solomon. Mike ran to Esau's side and knelt. Esau was dazed and bruised but alive. His hands were bound back of him and he had a purple welt on his forehead in addition to other injuries. His cotton shirt had been torn to tatters which hung from his belt. He was barefoot. If he had been carrying a weapon it had been taken from him. He was a massive man of ebony. Even in his dazed condition his mighty muscles worked on his powerful frame.

Mike looked up at the stevedores who had

retreated to the prow of the packet. "What happened to him?" he demanded.

"He was jest a smart nigger that didn't know his place," one said.

Mike drew his hiding knife and cut the thongs, freeing Esau's wrists. He began massaging the black man's forearms, fearing the circulation might have been impeded so long that Esau would be in danger of gangrene. But that proved groundless. Esau began to revive and mumble and try to arise.

Mike vaulted onto the dock and walked up the gangplank to the deck of the steamboat where the two grinning stevedores stood. Their grins faded suddenly. They tried to evade him, but too late. He seized them by their bushy hair and cracked their heads together with dazing force.

"Did you two have anything to do with it?" he gritted. They were tough river rats who bore the scars of hard lives. They tried to break free, kicking with thick-soled brogans and swinging fists. They were like two active water bugs. Mike's arms were longer, his strength greater. Again he brought their skulls together with a thud.

"So you *are* the ones!" he said.

The pair, still seeing stars, caved in. "It wasn't our doin', mister," one of them gasped. "Leggo. You've broke my haid. An' yo're breakin' my neck."

"Who did it?" Mike demanded.

"Them Army boys," the man gurgled. "From the way we heard it, he tried to make the cal'vry doctor go with him to tend his squaw who was bearin' a baby. He tried to draw a gun on the doc an' force him to go along, the way it was told to us. The soldiers had to tie him up an' keep him tied up. They brung him along with them back to the fort."

"When did this happen?"

"Today, I reckon. All I know is that the doc an' a couple squads o' cal'vry men, along with their horses, come aboard a couple hours ago down the river. They brung the black man with them, all trussed up. He had been mighty hard to handle. Some o' the cal'vry boys was mussed up considerable. Seems like the doc, along with a detail, had rode down the river to meet the gal he's marryin' so he could escort her an' her party in style off the boat when we reached the fort."

Mike released them and returned ashore. Esau was sitting up. Mike helped him to his feet. It was minutes before the black man recognized him. It was more minutes, with Mike walking him in a circle before his mind began to clear.

"Mike!" Esau finally mumbled. "Mike McVey! When? Whar?"

"You're at Flagg," Mike said. "They brought you here on the steamboat."

Full recollection came. "Ruth!" Esau exclaimed. "She's in need —"

"I know," Mike said.

"You've seen her?"

"Yes. Only a couple of hours ago. I came to the fort to find you and to fetch the doctor to her."

"How is she?" Esau demanded pleadingly.

When Mike did not answer at once Esau tried to read his expression. "She ain't — ain't bad, is she?" he asked.

There was no point in holding back the truth. "Things aren't good," Mike admitted. "You must get there as fast as you can. She needs you. That will help. She wants you. Take my horse. I gave him a hard ride getting here, so keep that in mind. But get there. I'll bring the doctor along later. He'll listen to reason, I'm sure."

"Doctor?" Esau spat the word with complete bitterness. "He's no doctor, else he'd act like one. He won't help. I rode to de fo't to git him, but he'd left with an escort o' soldiers to ride down de rivah an' meet de steamboat. Dey tol' me de woman he's goin' to marry would be aboard. I nigh killed my mule ketchin' up with him. He wouldn't listen to me. I got down on my knees to him. I begged. He jest turned an' walked away. I reckon I sort o' went out o' my haid. I tried to make him go with me. I drawed a gun. De soldiers jumped on me an' he tol' dem to tie me up. Dey hit me with somethin'. After dat I don' remember much 'til now."

Mike led Esau to where he had tethered the roan. The big man was still not too steady on his feet, and Mike had to help boost him into the saddle. He slapped the roan into motion.

"I'll bring the doctor," he repeated.

Esau was hanging to the horn as the horse carried him away along the trail that would lead him to his cabin.

Chapter 3

A steamboat from upriver was swinging toward the landing. It was the *Far Frontier*. Mike could see Pat Flannery handling the wheel personally, preparing to dock the craft alongside the *Far West*.

Mike left the riverfront and hurried up the path to the stockade gate of the fort. The troopers on guard there challenged him, then recognized him and let him pass. Two of them even saluted, although they gazed at his ragged buckskins, amazed. They had soldiered under him. In any event, it was a festive occasion and routine was abandoned for the night. Many civilians from the settlement were also streaming through the gate to take part in the festivities or merely to look on.

The regimental companies had been dismissed and the men were grouping around the long, log-built structure that flanked the parade grounds and was called the armory. It also served as the officers' recreation quarters and for formal affairs.

The armory was brilliant with light.

Music drifted from the open doors, produced by the horns and drums of a portion of the post band. Along with that came the sound of laughter and voices.

Mike pushed through the gaping soldiers until he could gaze through a window. A formal dinner was beginning. Colonel Cool sat at the head of a long banquet table which bore linen, silver and crystal. He was flanked by the four feminine guests. The officers of the post and their ladies sat in protocol order. A few civilian dignitaries from the settlement were relegated to the foot of the table.

Marsh Prine was at Cool's left. As the chief medical officer of the regiment, the insignia of his profession gleamed on the shoulders of his dress uniform. The coppery-haired girl was at his side. She was gay and gifted with laughter. Slightly freckled, she was obviously endowed with healthy vitality. She had hazel-green eyes in a good face that was handsome rather than beautiful. Beauty was the word that described the dark-eyed, dark-haired girl who had arrived with her on the packet and who now sat at the colonel's right. It had been a long time since Mike had seen a white woman, and he had never before seen two so exquisitely garbed and so radiant.

He appraised the situation. He had hoped he would be able to speak to Marsh Prine alone before the table was seated. That being impossible now, he had only one recourse. That was to stand in the wide doorway and beckon in the hope Prine would relent and leave the table to join him and give more consideration to his plea.

Troopers were on guard at the steps leading to the veranda that fronted the armory, but he bluffed them, with a return to his officer's training, into standing aside. He moved across the porch and through the door into the lamplight of the banquet room.

He had picked an unfortunate moment. Colonel Cool was rising to his feet, a wine glass poised, about to deliver the inaugural toast. He spotted Mike and froze in an awkward posture. Wine sloshed from his glass down the front of his dress jacket. Some of it descended on the bare shoulders of the coppery-haired girl, startling her.

Mike had a measure of revenge for the amusement his fall from his mount had aroused in her. Their eyes met and he could not help but wag his head in mock sympathy. He expected indignation and resentment. Instead, she smiled wryly, acknowledging that he had scored a point.

The colonel's reaction was considerably different. A choleric tide swelled above the collar of his jacket. He glared at Mike, so angry he was unable to speak for a moment. Mike realized that the chances of succeeding in his mission had been reduced to the vanishing point, if there had been any chance at all in the first place. Roscoe Cool might forgive some transgressions but never one against his dignity.

Marsh Prine was so taken aback by Mike's entrance and the disaster to the colonel that he, also, could only stare speechless. Mike still had to try. He owed that to Esau and Dawn-in-the-Sky. He walked down the room toward where Prine sat. The buzz of voices that had been aroused by the colonel's mishap faded. Silence spread along the table as the diners became aware of Mike's presence.

Mike bent close so that he could speak in Prine's ear. He was acutely aware of the nearness of the girl at Prine's left, aware of the healthy satin quality of the bare shoulder so close at hand, of the coppery hair that gave a faint fine fragrance.

"I'm asking you to do this as a personal favor, Marsh," he whispered. "Esau Solomon saved my life once, and nearly gave his own life to do it. You might be able to

41

save the life of his wife. I saw her. She needs you. She is going to die."

Prine tried to lean away from him. He was flushing and angry. "You fool!" he breathed. "Get out of here! What do you mean, trying to embarrass me in front of my fiancée?"

Colonel Cool found his voice. "Sergeant of the guard!" he roared, his voice climbing up the scale. "Throw this ruffian out of this place. Kick him out of the post and see to it that he is never allowed to enter the gates again."

Boots thudded on the floor as the guard came racing to obey. "Please, Prine!" Mike said desperately. "It will only take little more than an hour to get there."

Prine turned his head away, his lips stonily closed. Mike felt rough hands on his arms. He wrested away. "All right, Jenkins," he said to the sergeant with whom he was well acquainted. "I'll leave."

He walked down the room toward the door, surrounded by the soldiers. "I ought to have you thrown in the guardhouse, McVey!" the colonel raged. "I'll do exactly that if you show your face around Fort Flagg again."

Mike did not look back as he walked through the door out of the armory. There, on the wooden veranda, he came face-to-face with Pat Flannery, captain of the *Far Frontier*. The steamboat captain, who had just come ashore, was hurrying to join the banquet. He was freshly shaven and had donned a clean white shirt and tie and a brass-buttoned captain's jacket into which his hefty shoulders were crammed like the quarters of an overfed beef. He had waxed the ends of his sorrel-colored mustache. His bulbous red nose gleamed.

Mike's sudden appearance in his path was taken by Flannery as an intention to carry out the promise that had been made to pay him off for refusing to aid Esau's wife a few hours earlier. Flannery reacted instantly and violently.

"Ye scut!" he snarled and swung a fist. Mike was unprepared. Flannery's blow caught him on the jaw, hurling him back. He reeled past the arms of the surprised troopers and collided with diners at the banquet table.

Women screamed, men yelled in dismay. Mike found himself crashing to the floor amid flying skirts and petticoats and shattering glasses and tableware. The plump wife of Major Bart Anderson, the Post Adjutant, was one of the last to topple. She landed on Mike's stomach, driving the breath from him in a long *wh—sh.*

He managed to wriggle free of Hettie Anderson's weight and get to his feet. Flannery was standing aghast at the havoc, as though not believing he had accomplished so much with one punch.

Mike had enough strength left, even though Hettie Anderson had flattened him, to attempt to flatten Flannery. He swung straight and true to the burly man's ruddy jaw. The punch drove Flannery staggering. He shook off the effects and came bulling at Mike, head down, big fists mauling. Mike, outweighed forty pounds, was driven back. Slugging fiercely, locked in combat, they stumbled over Hettie, who was trying to get to her feet. This time both of them crashed into the table, spreading destruction farther along the board.

An avalanche of soldiers descended on them, obeying the colonel's incoherent screeching. They were dragged apart. Flannery's shirt and captain's regalia were stained with gore from a nose that was broken again.

"This divil came at me, Colonel!" he panted. " 'Twas only this evenin' he told me he'd try to waylay me the next time we met. Tis not me that was huntin' trouble. I was only defendin' meself."

"Throw that renegade into the guardhouse!" Cool yelled. "I'll see that he'll regret this outrage to his dying day."

The coppery-haired girl spoke. "Colonel, it seemed to me that this man you're ordering to the guardhouse didn't start this brawl. This other man hit him first, and without provocation as far as I could see."

"Provocation, is it?" Flannery moaned. "Beggin' your pardon, young lady, but did you not hear me say that he had only recently promised to assail me the next time we met. An' look at him. A renegade he is as the colonel says. An' a scoundrel. A cutthroat, likely, who would as soon kill me as talk about it. I was only taking precautions when I pushed him away from me. An' see what the scut has done to me. My poor nose. Broken it is. I'll be disfigured for life. For life, miss."

"On the other hand it may be an improvement," the girl said.

Colonel Cool angrily shouldered his way through the gaping officers and their ladies who had left the table and were grouped around Mike and the troopers. "Sergeant!" he frothed. "Are you going to obey an order or do you want to find yourself in the guardhouse along with this troublemaker?"

The troopers came to attention. They seized Mike and began to carry him bodily out of the banquet hall. "Set me down, you idiots!" he snarled and tore free of their grasp.

He marched with them across the parade ground to the squatty, log-built structure that served as a guardhouse. It was un-lighted. After some fumbling, a candle was ignited. By its light, Sergeant Pete Jenkins led him to one of the four cells and mo-tioned him to enter. He snapped a padlock that secured the door.

Before the detail left with the candle Mike saw that two of the other cells were empty. A drunken soldier was sprawled on the bunk of the fourth cell, snoring loudly.

Darkness closed in. He heard the tramp of boots as the troopers returned to duty at the banquet hall. There was muted snickering as they departed. It was a story that would be told and retold in barracks and bivouacs for years.

Mike groped his way to the bunk and sat down on the straw-stuffed pallet. He began to feel the effects of the hectic moments when he and Flannery had traded punches. Flannery had fought in the ring in his younger days under the rules where battles lasted sometimes for hours. His fists could still deal punishment, and Mike tenderly nursed a swollen jaw. That was where

Flannery's first punch had landed, and he decided he was lucky the jaw had not been broken or at least dislocated. He became aware of other souvenirs of the encounter. He had bruised and aching ribs and a stiffened left arm. The jaw had not been the only target of Flannery's clubbing fists.

He heard the footsteps of a sentry outside the barred window. "I could stand a drink," he called.

The soldier laughed. "So could I."

"I mean water," Mike said. "But I would settle for a good snort of red-eye."

The soldier left and presently returned. Entering the guardhouse, he pushed a tin of water through the mess trap. "Missouri River red-eye," he said. "Best I can do. If it was anybody but you, Mr. McVey, I wouldn't have bothered. It's ag'in guardhouse regulations."

Mike drank thirstily of the mud-flavored water. "Your voice is familiar," he said. "You're Sergeant Hank Craig."

"Private Craig," the man replied. "I didn't seem to git along so well after you pulled out. The colonel busted me down through corporal to buck, an' has kept me busted."

"You never were one to know enough not to speak his mind when he wasn't asked," Mike observed.

"Look who's talkin'!" Craig snorted. "You made yourself such a burr under the saddle the colonel was glad to git rid of you. Bein' a common soldier, I've got another year to go."

The music resumed at the armory. Order had been restored, and the banquet was being continued.

"Who are the young ladies?" Mike asked. "I understand one of them is marrying Marsh Prine."

"They're from somewhere back East. Wherever Dr. Prine came from. He went back there last fall an' got hisself officially engaged. I was told there'd been an understandin' between them for some time. She's a blueblood from the looks. I wish her luck. She might need it. Prine's a long way from bein' the worst I've run into in this man's army, but he's the kind you always salute, even though he's only a sawbones, else you're likely to find yourself pulling kitchen duty or walkin' nightguard for a month. Him an' the colonel see eye-to-eye."

"What's the bride's name?"

"Nancy Halstead, so I was told."

"That's the redhead? The green-eyed one?"

"I reckon. The other one's a cousin what came along to be best woman or whatever they call such people at weddin's. If you ask me, I'd be hard put to it to pick the purtiest of the two. Both of 'em are real lookers. The other two ladies air mothers or aunts, I take it. They all look like they're well fixed, by the way they dress. Marsh Prine knew what he was doin' when he went back East. He's fixin' to feather his nest. They say the father o' the Halstead gal is a big-wig back there. Swings a lot of weight. Prine's never been happy out here on the frontier. It's my guess he's goin' to be transferred, or maybe git out o' the service before long."

Craig asked if there was anything else he could do. Mike handed back the empty tin. "Plenty, but it'd cost you a jolt in a federal prison."

He added, as Craig started to leave, "I've been out of touch with things lately. Has there been any fighting with the tribes this year?"

"Nothin' to speak of," Craig said. "A few braves try to raid acrost the river now an' then, an' we chase 'em back. Ain't been a real campaign this year. Nothin' but garrison duty with the men gittin' fat an' lazy an' some tryin' to desert. Too much drill an' spit an' polish an' salutin'. But it suits the colonel."

"What are the reports from treaty country?"

"As long as they stay over there we leave 'em alone. But there's a rumble that Sheridan is pushin' to send in Custer an' the 7th to stir things up. There's a lot of pressure back in Washington to find out just what was signed away when they gave all that country over to the Sioux an' Cheyenne. Settlers are edgin' in from the Platte country to the south, an' pilin' up along the Missouri up in this country. Hide hunters are itchin' to git at the northern herd o' buffalo, for the pickin's are gittin' slim south o' the Platte. If Custer comes in with the 7th he'll set the pot boilin'. He always does. I say the whole danged country over there ain't worth fightin' for."

"Has it ever occurred to the colonel that the tribes know all this and might not wait to be smashed by Custer or any other general?"

"What do you mean?"

"What have Cool's scouts found out lately?"

"I ain't on the staff, mister. I'm only a common soldier. How would I know?"

"Don't tell me the Army's changed that much. Every man in the ranks knows everything the top man knows, usually before he knows it himself. I saw a lot of Indian sign west of the river. Tracks of big villages on the move."

"If'n I was you I wouldn't admit that I'd been in treaty country, Mr. McVey. He don't like you none an' he'd bring charges ag'in you. Anyway the scouts have already told him there are Indians in some numbers near the river. But all they're doin' is followin' a big herd o' buffalo that's driftin' north. They're movin' out of the colonel's territory."

The scouts probably were right. Still, an uneasiness remained in the back of Mike's mind. It was evident that discipline was lax at the fort. The post could be easy prey for a surprise attack. Still, Mike doubted that the tribes would break the treaty by crossing the Missouri in force.

The band at the armory struck up a cotillion. The banquet had ended and dancing was starting. Mike had marched and whirled and flirted with gay partners many times when he had been an officer in the regiment. He could visualize Roscoe Cool and his wife setting the style for thc cotillion, could imagine the glitter of swords and brass buttons, the swirl of silk and satin, the gleam of jewelry. The ladies of the post would hold back nothing in the way of display on this night. Even on the meager salaries their husbands were paid, military wives seemed to have a genius for being able to deck themselves out on festive occasions.

He pictured the coppery-haired girl, Nancy Halstead, in Marsh Prine's arms. "When is this wedding to take place?" he called.

"In a day or two," the sentry replied. "An' none too soon to please us soldiers. We've been drove like slaves fer a month, sprucin' up this post. You'd think he was marryin' the Queen o' Sheba."

The thought of the handsome, green-eyed girl marrying Marsh Prine rubbed against Mike's grain. Prine had his good points, no doubt, but Mike felt that she never had seen the reverse side of his nature, or had been blind to it. He pitied her.

His thoughts turned to his own problems and those of Esau Solomon. He feared that the guardhouse might be his residence for some time. He was at the mercy of Roscoe Cool. The colonel probably was exceeding his authority in placing Mike under military arrest, but, like all commanders of these isolated military posts, he was a law unto himself.

Cool was a political appointee who had been elevated to his rank during the Civil War where he had seen little or no combat, having been mainly engaged in liaison work between the field generals and War Department offices. He had engineered his appointment to the frontier over Phil Sheridan's opposition who knew him to be more concerned with parade etiquette and promotion rather than field duties.

Sheridan had assigned him to Fort Flagg, which, being on the east shore of the Missouri, was a less sensitive spot than some of the forts farther up the river which had been established on the west side, and were thorns in the sides of the tribes.

Roscoe Cool felt that it was beneath him to be stationed at a rude border post, but he had his heart set on wearing the stars of a general and knew that his best chance to win them was to gain recognition and publicity by leading his troops in combat. Now that the Civil War was long ended, about the only path was by killing Indians.

He had been balked by a War Department order forbidding campaigning across the river, except under great provocation. He had taken advantage of the "provocation" loophole in the order by seizing on an unverified report by a settler that the Sioux were raiding on the east side of the river. Refusing to listen to the advice of subordinates, Mike among them, who had experience at campaigning against the tribes, he had crossed the river with an inadequate force. The result was that he had been soundly trounced by the Sioux, and had been forced to retreat ignominiously across the river with nothing to show for the effort but dead and wounded men and loss of much equipment.

Mike had been the one who had most vigorously opposed the foray, pointing out there was nothing to back up the story the Sioux were raiding. The result was that he had cooled his heels on garrison duty at the fort and had missed being involved in the defeat.

A dozen young braves, scarcely more than boys, and two squaws, had been taken prisoner by Cool during the retreat. Cool had ordered them executed as revenge for the loss of his men, but Mike had seen to it that word was telegraphed to Sheridan at Omaha, who intervened in time and ordered the release of the captives. Sheridan had also ordered Cool's demotion from command at Fort Flagg, but higher powers had intervened at the White House and Cool had remained in charge.

He had made Mike's position so untenable, as a result, that resignation was the only answer. Sheridan, knowing the circumstances, had accepted his resignation and Mike had headed for Cheyenne, only to make his strike in treaty country.

Chapter 4

Lights from the armory where the music and dancing went on reached into the window of the guardhouse. Mike's eyes became tuned to the gloom, and he could make out the shape of the drunken soldier who still mumbled and snored in the cell across the way. Hank Craig's bootheels crunched monotonously on gravel outside the building as he paced his beat. Mike's jaw and ribs throbbed. The chill of the river reached into the guardhouse.

He morosely began reviewing his life which had led him here. He had enlisted in an Ohio regiment at the age of sixteen and had fought through the greater part of the war, the later two years in one of Sheridan's cavalry regiments. When mustered out after Appomattox, he was suffering from swamp fever as a result of the long campaign of the Wilderness, and carried the half-healed scars of two Confederate rifle balls. He still carried those scars as souvenirs of makeshift field surgery, done without opiates by harassed surgeons.

After a period of drifting as a civilian, he

had returned to the cavalry, enlisting in Sheridan's army of the west that guarded the Union Pacific construction and escorted settlers' wagons through the Platte Valley.

After that hitch he hunted buffalo for a summer on the Kansas plains but was horrified by the slaughter which was leading to the extermination of the herds. He had prospected in the Colorado gold country without luck. He finally reenlisted in the cavalry and took part in some of the campaigns against the Southern Cheyenne and the Sioux as far west as Cheyenne and south to Fort Dodge. It was Sheridan in person who had promoted him to a second lieutenancy, and then to first grade, and assigned him, later on, to Cool's regiment at Fort Flagg.

Although he had fought in wars and had hunted buffalo and had risked his scalp acting as lone envoy in Indian encampments, he was essentially an orderly man with disciplined plans for his future. Here and there he had met young ladies and had come within an ace of marrying one very fine brunette at Cheyenne. In fact she had been still somewhat in his mind when he had set out for Cheyenne that day last autumn.

His resignation from the Army and the

months of loneliness in the Indian country had settled his mind on one point at least. Never again would there ever be any thought of returning to the routine life of an obscure officer at a military post. He had seen too much of battle and of discipline. He was through with the Army, with the cavalry. He owed that much at least to Roscoe Cool.

He was thinking of the gold that lay hidden in the crevice of the gully near Esau's cabin. That warmed him, gave him the feeling of superiority over Cool, over everyone. He lived over again the tremendous bounding elation that had carried him to the heights when he had realized he had struck it rich. He had pursued the will-o'-the-wisp in Colorado and it had always eluded him. And then, when he wasn't even looking for gold, he had stumbled onto it.

It had been a wild, delirious existence with death's hand always on his shoulder. He remembered the occasion when a Sioux hunting party had camped within gunshot of the thicket into which he had crawled when he had heard the thud of approaching hoofs. They had bivouacked overnight so close he could hear their voices. Lucky for him, they had brought no dogs with them, or he would have surely been discovered and killed. And lucky for him, none had wandered down the stream from their camp, for he had been given no time to wipe out evidence of the panning he had been doing on a gravel bar.

There had been other narrow escapes previously, but that one was so harrowing it convinced him he had about run out his string. He had packed his gold on the ponies and had pulled out as soon as he considered it safe after the Sioux had gone on their way.

He kept telling himself that all the gold in the world was not worth what he had gone through. It had been even worse than the strain and terror of the Civil War. At least, in places such as Lookout Mountain and the Wilderness he had not been alone.

Still, another part of his mind kept urging him to go back. It kept reminding him he hadn't panned all of the creek and that there might be a bigger fortune awaiting him. As always, he faced the exact truth. It wasn't the wealth that was tempting him. He *wanted* to go back, *wanted* to live over those days of extreme peril.

Then came the mocking voice of his conscience. What about even the gold he had already found? There was still that jabbing belief that it should not be his and that he'd taken advantage of the Indians to pan it.

"You fool!" he told himself aloud. "It's yours!"

"What's that?" Hank Craig asked, peering through the bars of the window. "What did you say?"

"I said nothing," Mike answered. "You're imagining things, soldier."

He sat silent and depressed, almost frightened. Cool had called him a renegade. He looked down at his ragged garb of animal skins, stained with the grease and grime of many campfires. He fingered the buckskin band that kept his unruly dark hair out of his eyes.

He had become so accustomed to such garb that he hadn't realized what sort of an impression he would make. Now, that he had time to ponder it, he was confused. Was he really turning into one of those furtive hermits who preferred to rove the plains alone? That frightened him still more. Since he had made the gold strike he had been dreaming of himself as living in the lap of luxury. Wine, women, song! St. Louis, New Orleans, New York. Perhaps even Paris. A man could travel fast in those places, drink deep of the cup of life. Now it did not seem to matter.

It came to him that he had no future, no reason for anything. Except to drift as he had drifted since Appomattox. He had no family. His parents had died of hardship when he was a boy on a hardscrabble farm in the barren foothills of the Appalachians in southeastern Ohio. His two sisters had married farmers and had grown old long before their time, bearing children, and had gone to their graves, worn and willing to die at thirty. His only brother, older than he, had died in a Confederate prison camp after being captured at Chickamauga.

He thought of the coppery-haired girl. For him, all the faint, feminine laughter that drifted from the armory came from her lips. All the love of life, the beauty of existence, the richness of this evening, the promise of a lifetime of evenings, seemed embodied in her. And she belonged to Marsh Prine.

For the first time in his life Mike McVey, born with a rusty spoon in his mouth, knew savage envy, molten resentment of the luck of another man. This Nancy Halstead was the kind of a woman who should belong to him. Gay, beautiful, lighthearted, sure of herself, intellectual, no doubt, she would also, no doubt, be only highly amused at the thought of sharing a life with a ragged, bearded, buckskin-clad plainsman. Who was he, Mike McVey, to even think of the delicate perfume that had come from her hair? Who was the likes of he to remember the soft rustle of her skirt as she passed by when she had come down the gangplank on the colonel's arm, radiant and gorgeous?

Remembering his cached gold, he laughed cynically. At least he could buy pretty women, likely even women of culture with the tilt of snobbery in them. He might even buy a woman somewhere who had coppery gold hair and hazel-green eyes. But Marsh Prine would have the one whose image was before him, mocking him with her inaccessibility.

The tap of approaching bootheels sounded, along with the creak of a sword belt. An officer's voice spoke crisply. "Is that you, Craig? Release McVey.

"Colonel's orders," the arrival added. Mike identified the voice as belonging to Lieutenant George Willis, who had been a fellow officer in the regiment.

"He's to be marched out of the post and warned that it will go hard with him if he shows his face here again," George Willis continued. "Fetch the sergeant at arms and tell him to bring a candle. It's black as the second pit around here."

Presently more footsteps came on the double. A candle was lighted and men entered. The padlock on Mike's cell was freed and the barred door opened.

Mike emerged and said, "Thank you kindly, George. Did you put in a good word for me with the colonel?"

George Willis laughed hollowly. "I'm not in the habit of putting my head in the lion's mouth, Mike. Don't waste your thanks on me. I only follow orders around here and toe the chalk line the colonel draws. You are indebted to one of the young ladies. Miss Halstead. She prevailed on the colonel to turn you loose, though why a beauty like that would waste her pity on a man who looks like a shipwrecked pirate is beyond me, 'specially when I'm around. She didn't want any shadow to mar the occasion."

"I see," Mike said. "Sort of emptying the jails of the scoundrels to show how magnanimous the queen can be. In view of the fact I have a very important matter to take care of, give Miss Halstead my compliments and my thanks and my best wishes. Tell her I hope to be able to repay this kindness some day."

"You'd be thrown back into the guardhouse and I'd be sent to Siberia if I carried such a message and the colonel found out about it," Willis said. "Don't look a gift horse in the teeth. I'd advise you, as a friend, to clear out before the colonel changes his mind."

"I'd like to borrow a horse, George. I loaned mine to Esau Solomon so he could get to his wife's side."

"You don't really think the colonel would let me or anyone else let you take Army property off the post, do you? Where do you intend to ride, by the way?"

"To Esau's place."

"I was afraid so. I don't hold with Marsh Prine's refusal to at least try to do what he could for the Cheyenne girl. He's a doctor and they take some sort of an oath to help humans in need. I understand that they treated that black man mighty rough, slugging him and tying him up on board a packet when all he wanted was help for his squaw. But, if you're of a mind to throw in with him I'm afraid you'll have to walk. I wouldn't dare get a horse for you."

George Willis turned and walked away, heading back to the festivities at the armory, washing his hands of Mike's affairs. The sergeant and Hank Craig marched Mike to the stockade gate. "You heard the colonel's orders, sir," the sergeant said. "Us men in the ranks would appreciate it if you didn't try to make any more trouble for us."

Left alone, Mike debated his course. He

considered going to the civilian settlement beyond the post and try to borrow a horse, but decided there would be little or no chance anyone there would trust a gaunt, bearded, ragged man who was branded as a renegade by the post commander.

So he did as George Willis had advised. He set out on foot to cover the ten-mile trail to Esau's place. He traveled at a jog part of the time, but was forced to slow to a walk often to give his lungs and body a respite. An intuitive dread of what he might find at Esau's place kept him going to the point of exhaustion.

His fears were borne out. He was nearing the clearing when he heard the dreary keening of Indian women. It was their lamentation for the dead.

He slowed and walked into the clearing. No light showed at Esau's cabin, but from it came the wailing and weird chanting. Moving nearer, he saw that half a dozen Indian women were huddled in the open near the doorway and uniting in the lamentation. More of Dawn-in-the-Sky's relatives or friends had been summoned after he had left for the fort, or, more probably, had been camped in hiding nearby.

He peered around. "Esau!" he called.

The wailing of the squaws stilled for a moment, then resumed. "Esau!" he spoke again.

A shadow moved from the deeper shadow of the cabin. Esau came into the moonlight and stood motionless — a great, black rock of a man. He had removed the tatters of his shirt and was bare to the waist. He had tied a buckskin thong around his head. In that was thrust a feather.

"Ruth?" Mike asked.

"She gone," Esau said. "The Great Spirit, he take her."

"The Lord has taken her," Mike said. "We're both sure of that, aren't we? I'm very sorry, Esau. Very, very sorry."

He extended a hand. Esau ignored it. "De yellaleg doctah might have kept Ruth with me," he said. "He could have come an' tried to help her. But he wouldn't."

Mike had no answer for that, no way of solacing the grief that tore at the big man. He started to move toward the door of the cabin, but Esau barred his way. "No, Mike," Esau said. "My people will take care o' her. Dey will prepare her to ride up de Great Medicine Road into de sky. She will wait dare 'til I join her."

"The baby?" Mike asked.

Esau remained silent. Mike knew then that the baby was dead also.

"It better dat you go away, Mike," Esau said.

Mike understood. Esau wanted no one to witness the anguish he suffered. Mike looked at the feather in Esau's headband. "That doesn't belong there," he said.

"I'm Cheyenne now, if'n dey'll have me," Esau said. "Her people are my people."

Then he was gone, walking away and merging with the black shadows. The keening of the Indian women went on and on, the sound rising and falling.

Mike stood there for a time, his eyes moist, an uncontrollable tightness in his throat. He, too, was mourning Dawn-in-the-Sky, mourning the lost brightness that had been hers, remembering her love of laughter, her tenderness toward the big black man.

He found himself listening with increasing intensity to the chanting of the squaws. There was a primitive quality to it that found a deep response within him. It fitted in with the night and the tragedy that had come to this wild place. He forced himself to stop listening. That required an effort of will, almost a physical force. Again he felt fright. Once more he was asking himself if he was really becoming what Colonel Cool and Marsh Prine and George Willis believed — an outcast — a renegade — perhaps an ally of the Sioux.

He called Esau's name once more but no response came from the dark shadows. He gave it up and turned away. He found the roan, dropping with weariness, tethered at the corral gate, still saddled. The Indian women had placed his two pack ponies in the enclosure. He stripped the rigging from the roan and turned it into the corral also. The remains of a stack of wild hay stood near and he tossed in armloads.

The Indian women had left his camp pack near the corral. He carried it to a dry sandbar in the channel of the river and built a fire of dry twigs. He spread his tarp and worn blanket and buffalo robes.

He carried pemmican in his parfleche bags, along with dry, hard biscuits and coffee beans. The Crow wife of the Canuck trader whom he had visited for supplies had taught him how to make pemmican of shredded buffalo haunch into which was pounded tallow, dried wild cherries, salt and a touch of cayenne. When cured it became so hard it took strong jaws to masticate it, but when warmed into stew or in a skillet it was more easily handled. It was enormously nourishing, but not exactly appetizing.

He shaved scraps of the pemmican into

the skillet, added biscuits, flour and water, and boiled coffee from beans he mashed on a flat stone with the hand ax.

He finally settled down to sleep, his warsack for a pillow and the wailing of the squaws still faintly in his ears. He was beginning to drift off to sleep when he thought of his gold. He was startled. How could he have forgotten it for so many hours? It had been the pulse of his life for so many months. He had lived with it, worked with it, thought of nothing else. Yet it had been totally out of his mind.

This annoyed him. But he was more puzzled than annoyed. Once again he was realizing that there were things about this Michael McVey, whose character he was beginning to really examine for the first time in his life, that he did not know, did not understand.

Sleep eluded him for a long time. He lay listening to the mourning of the squaws and thinking of Esau. Finally he slept. He partially awakened, believing the earth had communicated the sound of horses. These faded and he slept again.

The morning star was flaming in the sky and the horizon was brightening with the coming of day when he awakened suddenly and completely. Except for the murmur of the nearby river there was no sound. The keening of the Indian women was only a memory of a night that was ended. He rolled out of his robes, and dressed. Scaling the cutbank, he walked across the flat toward the cabin. It was a dark, unlighted shape in the chill of dawn. Finally he stood before the structure. Its slab door stood open, sagging on its leather hinges. He moved to the door, fumbled for his tin of matches and got one lighted.

Esau's cabin was empty. The pallet where Dawn-in-the-Sky had lain was gone. All personal effects were gone. Only the rough table and benches that Esau had whipsawed and carpentered together with pegs were left in the place. The ashes in the fireplace where meals had been cooked were gray and dying.

Lying on the table was the Bible he had given Esau, its pages dog-eared, its leather binding worn from much use. A knife had been driven entirely through the book with such force it had split the plank in the tabletop beneath. The knife had been withdrawn.

Mike backed out of the place. He found himself almost wanting to run as he retreated to his camp. Esau had been an intensely religious man, starting his day each morning with thanks to the Creator for his existence. He had personally baptized Dawn-in-the-Sky at the time he had given her the name of Ruth in place of the colorful term her Cheyenne mother had chosen for her.

Mike could guess what had happened. They had taken Dawn-in-the-Sky away on her death pallet to where her people would perform their rites for the departed. Then Esau would enshrine her body in some secret place whose location no person but himself would know. That place, Mike was certain, would be across the river, in Indian country, Cheyenne country.

And Esau himself? The pierced Bible on the table gave the answer. It was bitter evidence that Esau was renouncing all the ways of the past. He had often gone among the Sioux and the Cheyenne, preaching peace and trying to show them that warfare was not the answer to their problems. He had believed that goodness and compassion on both sides was the solution, and had so impressed many of the chiefs that they had stayed the hands of their warriors on numerous occasions when scores of lives of white men and women would have paid the penalty. Now, it was evident, Esau had crossed the river.

The dawn had strengthened. The plains

were taking on the ruddy hue of life. Mike had lived on pemmican, buffalo and elk meat, hardtack biscuits and prairie chicken for weeks. He had been looking forward to the fare Esau would have provided. He opened Esau's smokehouse and found a side of bacon and a supply of smoked buffalo tongue, along with a bag of hominy hung above reach of the packrats. Returning to the river, he searched along its bank. Esau had always kept a trotline in the stream in order to add fish to his fare. A fishbox was sunken in the water, with rocks for weights. It contained half a dozen catfish of the small size that was sweet and delectable, left from Esau's last run of his line.

Returning to the cabin, he located the trap that led to the root cellar. A few potatoes and turnips remained of last year's crop. The potatoes were sprouting but were still firm and crisp, as were the turnips.

Mike built a cookfire. A big cookfire, indulging in that luxury that had been denied him for months. He boiled potatoes and turnips, he fried catfish with bacon. He ate. And ate. Even the coffee in his tincup seemed to have a new marvelous aroma.

The sun came up, warming the world. He lingered on his spread robe, drinking coffee, lulled by the music of the river. He was reluctant to face his problem. That problem lay nearby in the crevice in the gully. Its solution had seemed simple when he had viewed from afar during his journey from the Black Hills. It had been in his mind that he would merely take passage with his gold on some packet bound downriver from Fort Flagg, or perhaps from one of the other military posts down the river.

Now, face-to-face with the decision, he realized that he had been deluding himself, evading the truth. He had kept assuring himself that some easy plan would occur to him for spiriting his gold aboard, disguised or otherwise, without revealing its true nature, or, above all, its origin. None had occurred. He now had to admit the difficulties — the impossibility, rather. Once he let the secret slip out, the thing he had vowed to his infernal conscience to prevent, would take place. A stampede into the tribal hunting grounds would start.

Fort Flagg, above all, was impossible to him now as an embarkation point since his new difficulties with Colonel Cool. He was also dismally certain that he would be equally unwelcome at other posts down the river, and also a subject of suspicion, for Roscoe Cool would undoubtedly see to it that word of what had happened at Flagg would be known by telegraph to the commanders of other posts.

He tamped tobacco into his battered pipe and touched a match to it. It wasn't really tobacco. It was what the Indians called kinnikinik, a mixture of the bark of the red willow and strong tobacco. In Mike's pouch, the mixture was mainly willow bark, for tobacco had become a scarce luxury with him and was to be used only sparingly.

The more he thought of his situation the more ludicrous it became. He sat tossing pebbles into the rushing Missouri, and ruefully considered the habit Michael McVey had of getting himself into vexing predicaments.

Most men would have swaggered into Flagg with two ponies loaded with gold, told Roscoe Cool to go to hell, bought drinks for the settlement and for every soldier who dared risk Cool's wrath. That's what most men would have done. Even Roscoe Cool wouldn't dare throw into the guardhouse a man worth a small fortune, and, furthermore a man who knew where others might get rich.

That was where his blasted conscience came in, his silent obligation to the tribes.

"If I was really a man," he groaned aloud, "I'd throw the damned stuff into the river.

Then I'd be able to live with myself."

But he knew he couldn't bring himself to it. That was where avarice came in. Human avarice.

"What would you throw into the river?" a voice asked.

He rolled to his feet, all the lethargy gone. He was reaching for his rifle and preparing to duck, evade or meet a foe with whatever weapon he was likely to be facing.

Instead, he found himself confronted only by an unarmed young woman. She was the coppery-haired girl whom he had been told was to wed Marsh Prine — Nancy Halstead. In the background on the rim of the cutbank four mounted cavalry-men in charge of Sergeant Pete Jenkins waited, holding a sleek chestnut mare equipped with a sidesaddle.

Nancy Halstead was eying Mike with frowning speculation. She was wearing a dark riding habit, polished boots, with a riding derby held to her hair by a chinstrap.

Mike had snatched up the rifle. He lowered it, scowling. His scowl was for his own carelessness. The chatter of the river had helped smother the sounds of their approach, but it had been mainly his preoccupation with his problems that had thrown him off guard.

"I'm sorry," the young lady said. "I didn't

mean to startle you. Do you really have to glare at me like that?"

"You *could* have been a Sioux," Mike said.

"What is it you were telling yourself you ought to throw into the river?" she asked.

"Now, that's for me to know," Mike said. "Don't you ever talk to yourself?"

"Of course," she said. "I suppose everyone does."

Her gaze was traveling over him repeatedly. She seemed puzzled, unable to answer some question.

"What is it?" Mike asked.

"Well," she said frankly, "I'm a little surprised at finding an educated man under such a surface. However, I remember now that the colonel said you were an officer in the cavalry. You were cashiered for refusing to obey orders or something like that, I believe."

"You heard wrong, but it doesn't matter," Mike said.

"You certainly caused a lot of trouble at the fort last evening," she said.

"I understand you interceded for me and got me released from the guardhouse," Mike said. "For that I thank you." He indicated the four waiting troopers. "Where are the others?"

"Others?"

"That fool didn't let you come this far from the fort with only four soldiers to look after you, I hope."

"Are you referring to Colonel Cool?" she demanded.

"Well, there are a lot of fools around here, but he comes first on the list."

She tried to wither him with a tilt of her small nose and a glance from frigid eyes. "Colonel Cool says there's no danger this close to the fort. On this side of the river, in fact."

Seeing the look on Mike's face she hastily added: "As a matter of fact, the colonel really doesn't know I intended to come here. I didn't mention it. I told him I was only going for a short canter."

She paused a moment, waiting for him to speak. When he did not, she said, "Is there?"

"Is there what?"

"Any — any chance of — of —"

Mike turned and lifted his voice. "Jenkins! Come here, on the double!"

Sergeant Pete Jenkins reluctantly dismounted, turned the reins over to one of the troopers and came closer. He was beefy, red-eared and his manner was apologetic.

"Jenkins, you idiot, you ought to be busted down to private for this," Mike said. "You know blasted well that Sioux are always slipping across the river. They'd like nothing better than a chance like this."

"I'm sorry, sir," Jenkins mumbled. "The young lady wouldn't have it no other way. She said she'd find this place alone. I didn't figure my orders covered fetchin' her back to the post under guard an' by force."

"Don't blame the sergeant," Nancy Halstead said. "I badgered him into it. In fact I gave him the impression the colonel had understood that I wanted to come to this place."

"All right, Pete," Mike said, "but you should know enough about women, having been married a couple of times, to know she was running a high blaze on you."

Jenkins hurried back to the safety of his detail of troopers and mounted. Nancy Halstead was eying Mike again from head to foot, her nose wrinkled in disdain.

"For a former Army officer you look like you'd fallen out of a ragbag," she commented. "What are you, a spy, or something in disguise?"

"These," Mike said sourly, "are my Sunday best, at least until I can find time to visit a mercantile. However, we'll discuss high fashion some other time. The question is, why did you want to come here?"

She pointed toward Esau's shack. "I believe that is where the colored man lives, is it not?"

"It was."

"You mean he's not there. He has gone? What about the Indian girl? His wife? The one you told Dr. Prine was in need of help?"

"Is that why you came here?" Mike demanded incredulously. "You don't mean to tell me you were actually concerned about an Indian squaw?"

"I've done some hospital work among disabled veterans of the war. I've acted as midwife a time or two among their wives. I thought I might be able to help if I could."

Mike eyed her with sudden respect, for he knew she was sincere. "I'm sorry to tell you that you've wasted your time," he said. "It's ended."

She peered at the deserted shack and understood. "When?"

"It was all over when I got here last night."

"Then — then even Marsh would have been too late —" she began. She broke off, again seeing the hardening of Mike's expression.

"What about — about the baby?" she asked reluctantly. Mike shook his head. She winced a little. "What happened to the black man?" she asked. "His house seems deserted."

"He's gone with the Cheyenne. Dawn-in-the-Sky will be given a funeral somewhere, along with the baby, in the Indian fashion. Esau will bury them in a place of his own choosing."

"Dawn-in-the-Sky? Isn't that a beautiful name? How old was she?"

"Maybe nineteen. Maybe younger."

"So young! So young to die. Was she good looking?"

"I thought so. I thought she was beautiful. Esau thought she was the most gorgeous thing that ever had existed. He believes she had the right to stay alive."

"You're blaming Marsh, aren't you?" she exclaimed. "After all, he probably could not have done anything. Doctors can't perform miracles."

"He will have to live with the knowledge that he didn't try," Mike said. He added, "And so will his wife."

He wished in the next instant he hadn't said that. It was like the bite of a lash in her face. She turned and moved to her horse. "We'll go back to the fort, Sergeant," she said to Jenkins.

The sergeant helped her mount. "Hold it a minute, Pete," Mike said. "I'll saddle up and ride with you for a while. Five will be better than four."

"That won't be at all necessary," Nancy Halstead protested stiffly.

"Mr. McVey knows best, missy, if you don't mind me sayin' so," Jenkins said. "He's had considerable experience with Indians."

"So I understand," she said.

Mike rigged the roan, mounted and joined the group. Nancy Halstead ignored him. Taking the lead, he avoided the trail, feeling that if there was any chance of an ambush it would be waiting along the customary route. He guided the way across open flats where there were few places for scalp hunters to hide. Jenkins let him have the authority as a matter of course.

However, the trip was uneventful. Mike pulled up when the settlement and fort were only a mile or so away. "I'll head back now," he said. He spoke to Nancy Halstead. "I wish you the best of luck and happiness, Miss Halstead."

Before she could answer he turned and rode away. When he looked back she was riding toward the fort with the troopers.

Chapter 5

Returning to his camp, Mike again grappled with the problem of getting his gold out of the country. He debated the possibility of building another raft and floating down the river with his fortune until he reached more civilized country. He quickly ruled against that plan. It would mean risking his three hundred pounds of gold to the vagaries of the Missouri. Literally putting all his golden eggs in one basket. That was unthinkable after what he had been through to get it this far.

He remembered that Esau had built a flatboat with which to fish and run his trotline. He searched along the brush of the river's margin and found the craft moored with a long line in hiding under the overhang of willows. It was a heavy boat with holes bored for thole pins. Its oars were missing, but Mike believed they probably were at Esau's cabin.

He studied it for a time, then ruled against risking his gold in that manner also. He knew the river, the wild, unpredictable Missouri. It would mean days of constant toil and tension, miles of hand roping down rough stretches which he would not dare try to navigate in a heavily laden flatboat.

There was only one way and that was to continue by saddleback and pack. He settled on it with complete lack of enthusiasm. He'd had his fill of that sort of thing after so many weeks of it, so many miles. It meant more weeks of it, more hundreds of miles, for he was realizing now that he might have to travel as far as Council Bluffs before attempting to turn his dust into cash. Council Bluffs and Omaha bankers handled much raw gold which flowed back from California and Nevada over the rails of the Union Pacific. He would not have to answer pointed questions about the source of his strike in those busy communities.

But that journey held no allure for him, not only because of the continued hardships of roughing it, but for the fact that he would have to continue sleeping with an eye open and an ear cocked. Perhaps the hazards would be even greater. The Indian danger would lessen as he progressed toward his goal, but it would be replaced by another. The border swarmed with outlaws and opportunists who preyed on lone travelers. A man with two loaded pack ponies, when one usually was sufficient, would be cause for comment — and investigation.

He decided to put off the final reluctant decision until morning at least, for he wrestled with his problem longer than he realized. The sun was low in the sky. He built a supper fire, cooked another meal in the dusk, finished it and scoured the skillet and tinware.

He doused the fire with river water and carried his bed and tarp to a new location well away from his camp. He had turned his horses into Esau's corral for the night. If any Indians were on this side of the river and had been watching, hoping to surprise him in his sleep, they'd have to do some stalking.

He had slept only a few hours when the ground beneath him communicated the sound of hoofbeats, moving fast. Many hoofs. He rolled out of his blankets, reached for his rifle and sat waiting and listening.

The pound of hoofs became a steady rumble. He heard an officer shout a command to halt with the noncoms passing the word along. The flat where Esau's cabin stood became alive with movement. Bull's-eye lanterns sent shafts of light through the night.

"Come out of there, nigger!" a voice shouted hoarsely.

Mike realized that was Roscoe Cool, himself, speaking. The activity had centered around Esau's cabin.

The butt of a rifle pounded on a door, the sound booming loudly in the night. Mike heard the door flung open. Sounds indicated that several soldiers had rushed into the place.

"There ain't nobody here, sir," a soldier reported. "Looks like he heard us comin', an' lit out."

"Scatter!" the colonel roared. "He might be hiding around here. Search the brush. Round the devil up. But no shooting."

Cool's voice had lost its customary icy precision and was shrill with rage and frustration. "Set fire to that damned shack and everything else on this place," he continued. "It'll give us light. Maybe it'll smoke him out. But be careful. No shooting, I say. He might have the lady with him."

Soldiers began racing through the land where Esau was preparing his garden. Mike could hear others shaking the sodden cornshocks.

The presence of three horses in the corral was reported to Cool. Mike heard the colonel ride to the enclosure, and could see the beams of bull's-eye lanterns following the animals as they milled around.

"Haven't I seen that roan somewhere not

long ago?" Cool was saying. "I remember now — that renegade, McVey, was riding a roan last evening at the landing. So he's had a hand in this outrage?"

Mike knew it was time to appear. He would be discovered sooner or later as the search widened. He buckled on his holstered pistol and left his covert, the rifle slung under his arm. He walked into the clearing.

Troopers, both afoot and mounted, came rushing upon him, sabers in their hands. "Take it easy, soldiers," Mike said. "This is Mike McVey. What's all the excitement about? Didn't I hear my name mentioned a moment ago?"

"This way, Colonel!" one of the troopers shouted. "We've got somebody!"

Roscoe Cool came spurring his horse to the scene. Flames were bursting from Esau's cabin, lighting the flat. Cool leaned from the saddle, peering. He had his sword in his hand, and Mike braced himself, preparing to parry the weapon with his rifle for he believed it was in the man's mind to cut him down where he stood.

Cool thought better of it and fought for control of his fury. "What in hell's flames are you doing here, you scoundrel?" he rasped. "Talk! And talk fast."

Marshall Prine, on foot, came running up. He burst through the circle of troopers that was gathering and hurled himself at Mike, attempting to seize him by the throat. "Where is she?" he screeched. "What has that black devil done with her?"

Mike wrested free so violently Prine was unbalanced and staggered to his knees. He fumbled for his pistol which was held by the closed flap of a cavalry holster.

Mike, leaping in, seized his arm, holding him helpless. "Are you drunk, Prine?" he gritted. "What are you trying to do — murder me? What are you talking about?"

"Don't try to pretend you weren't in on it!" Prine frothed. "Where's Nancy Halstead and that nigger? He sneaked into the fort tonight and tried to kill me! He kidnaped Nancy when she wouldn't let him shoot me down!"

Mike stood for a long moment, gripping Marsh Prine. He looked up, stunned, at Roscoe Cool. "What was that he said?" he asked.

"You heard him!" the colonel snarled. "This man, Esau Solomon, tried to murder Dr. Prine tonight at the fort. Miss Halstead happened to be passing near the door of the doctor's quarters and heard what was going on. She burst in, in time to save the doctor's

86

life. Then your black friend thought of a better thing. He knocked the doctor unconscious, left him tied and gagged, and made off with Miss Halstead."

"No!" Mike said numbly. "Not Esau Solomon! He wouldn't do a thing like that. He wouldn't kidnap a woman."

"He would and he did," Cool raged. "He told Dr. Prine he held him responsible for the death of his squaw and their baby. He said he'd make Dr. Prine pay. He tried to force Dr. Prine into fighting a duel with him. A duel to the death. When that didn't work, he carried Miss Halstead away."

Mike released Marshall Prine. Prine got to his feet. Now he managed to get out his pistol. He cocked it and jammed the muzzle against Mike's chest. "Where are they, McVey?"

"I don't know," Mike said. "How should I? This is all news to me."

"You lie! You were in cahoots with him. Talk or I'll blow your heart out."

"Put that gun down," Mike said. "Quit babbling and talk sense. I tell you I know nothing about any of this."

"Easy, Doctor," Cool said. He dismounted and pushed Prine's pistol away from Mike's chest. "I can't blame you for wanting to pull the trigger. We'll make this fellow tell what he knows. McVey, if you weren't in on this thing, why were you skulking around here?"

"Skulking isn't the word," Mike said. "I was camped here and siwashing out in the brush, so that just in case a Sioux happened to have spotted my campfire. Esau's wife was dead when I got back here from the fort last night. So was the baby. A bunch of Dawn-in-the-Sky's relatives, including her mother and sister were here. Sometime during the night while I was asleep they pulled out, taking the bodies with them."

"What did that black scoundrel say to you?"

"He was heartbroken," Mike said. "A man might say things he didn't really mean at a time like that."

"Then he *did* blame me!" Marsh Prine raged. "You heard him, didn't you? You knew he was out to kill me, but you didn't try to stop him."

"Esau is my friend," Mike said. "He made no threats to kill you, Prine, at least in my presence. I haven't seen him or talked to him since I got here late last night and found that his wife and baby had died."

"Why didn't you follow them when you found out they'd cleared out?"

"Why should I? It's bad medicine to go

where you're not wanted at a time like that in the way the tribes look at it."

"Bosh!" Colonel Cool snorted. "You're only trying to protect Solomon. You know more about this than you pretend. You always were fast with excuses. And you always were on the side of the Indians. That's why you were cashiered out of the Arm—"

"Not cashiered!" Mike snapped. "Not by you or by anybody. I left the Army of my own free will."

"Well, you *should* have been kicked out!" Cool said. "You might have had some of my superior officers fooled, but I know you for what you really are — a turncoat at heart. You've always been an Indian-lover."

"Sir!" Marshall Prine pleaded. "Make him tell what happened to Nancy. *Make* him talk."

"You fool!" Mike said. "Do you think I'd have hung around here if I'd have had any hand in stealing a white woman? Use what few brains you have."

He turned to Cool. "If Esau Solomon really kidnaped Miss Halstead I'll be the first to turn heaven and hell to try to get her back. Esau must have gone out of his head. He's a religious man. A good man. He'll come to his senses. I can't believe he'd harm an innocent young woman."

"Arrest him, Colonel!" Prine demanded. "He's only stalling, trying to give Solomon more time to get away. Make him tell what he knows."

"Sure!" Mike said. "Arrest me. Put me in solitary on bread and water. Wet blankets. A bucket of water on my head every hour to keep me cool. You know you're wrong when you say I'm in cahoots with the Indians, Colonel. I know their faults and they've got plenty to answer for. They'd kill me as soon as anyone if they got the chance. They've got reason to hate and distrust my kind of people. They've done wrong, but a lot of wrongs have been done them. I'm not on their side. Only on the side of right. Esau wasn't on their side either. At least not until all this happened. Now I'm not so sure."

"He's still only wasting time, Colonel!" Prine raged.

"I tell you that if Esau really took the young lady with him she won't be harmed," Mike said. "That's the only thing I can be sure about. He just isn't that kind."

"What do you mean, he isn't that kind? Didn't you just hear the colonel tell how he tried to kill me? He would have done it if Nancy hadn't interfered. Does that sound as though he wouldn't harm anybody?"

"I said he wouldn't harm *her*," Mike said. "He had nothing against her. It might be different where you're concerned, Marsh. He lost the one thing in the world that he really loved, the one thing that made life worth living for him. I'm afraid he might have taken her away from you to make you suffer the way he has suffered." He paused, then added, "Or for another reason."

"What would that be?" Prine demanded.

Mike didn't answer. It seemed to him none was needed. It should be clear to Prine that Esau Solomon might expect a man whose prospective bride was stolen to try to pursue her kidnaper and take vengeance, as well as rescuing his beloved. He didn't have the heart to point out this aspersion on Prine's courage here in the presence of others.

"When we catch this man," Roscoe Cool said, "he'll learn what suffering really is. Hanging's the best that will happen to him. If he's harmed her, he'll beg to be hanged before we are through with him."

He added, "And you too, McVey, if it turns out that you've really helped him in this dastardly thing."

"Let's talk facts," Mike said. "As I said, if Esau went out of his head from grief, he'll come to his senses. It's possible I might be able to find him and bring the lady back."

"We don't need your help!" Prine snarled.

"I think you do. It's my guess that Esau has crossed the river. I know the country over there. I'll have a better chance of finding him than anyone."

"I'm sure you would," Cool said bitingly. "I'm also sure you know the country. I've heard rumors that you were over there. You showed up at the trading post of that French-Canadian squawman a couple of times last winter. What were you doing in treaty country all that time if you weren't hanging around with the Sioux or the Cheyenne?"

"I was doing some hunting," Mike said. "Whether you agree or not, I'm going to cross the river and try to find Esau and the young lady."

"I have a better plan," Cool said. "You're crossing the river, right enough. But under arrest. This knowledge of the country that you mentioned might be very useful to me."

"If you mean what I think you mean, Colonel, you better forget it," Mike said. "I'm going over there alone. That's the only way it can be done."

"You're mistaken," Cool said. "I'm bringing up the command. I intend to make a sweep across the river that will turn up this black man — and you're going with me, either willingly, or as a prisoner."

"That might be the biggest mistake of your life," Mike said. "There are a lot of Indians over there, and not too far away. Maybe they've only moved in to hunt buffalo that are supposed to have drifted in along the river. Maybe they've got something else in mind."

"Are you trying to frighten me?"

"Yes, and you better be frightened, Colonel. I crossed the sign of some pretty big villages on the move. Hunting parties they might be, but they had children and big lodges with them in addition to the squaws, as far as I could see. Hunting parties like that turn into war parties in a hurry. You could find yourself in a hornet's nest."

He knew he had hit Cool's vulnerable spot. There was nothing Cool would like better than to restore prestige that he had lost in his debacle the previous summer. A successful sweep would do much to make amends and move him ahead toward the general's stars he coveted, particularly if he managed the rescue of the stolen girl. Her kidnaping from a post he commanded was already working against him, he knew. Her rescue would be dramatic and receive great publicity in Eastern papers. But defeat would be another matter.

"In addition, Colonel," Mike added, "if you go over there in force you might be signing Miss Halstead's death warrant. You know what usually happens to white captives in Indian villages when the troops attack."

Cool was backed into a corner. He stood scowling. "Did I understand you to say that you could find Miss Halstead and bring her back unharmed?" he finally demanded.

"Certainly not," Mike replied. "What I said was that I might have a better chance than anyone. After all, I was Esau's friend. I was also the friend of his wife. I knew her mother, Elk Woman. I've smoked the pipe with her father, Gray Buffalo. Not that he wouldn't kill me as he'd swat a fly if the card turned that way. But you never know what an Indian thinks. I might have a chance."

"She's dead already, no doubt," Cool said.

"There's always that possibility. At least it would be well to know, one way or another, for the sake of her relatives and friends."

"I suppose it would be the last I'd ever see or hear of you if I let you wriggle your way out of my fingers," Cool said.

"It could turn out that way," Mike said grimly. "I just mentioned that it's unlikely

I'd be welcomed with open arms by the Cheyenne. They distrust white men and have a habit of acting unpleasantly and in a hurry. I'm banking on one hole card. Esau Solomon."

"In what way?"

"He might stay their hands. And I believe, for the same reason, Miss Halstead is still alive and unharmed. The Cheyenne know him and trust him. He married into their tribe. She is his prisoner and he should have the say as to how she is treated. He's not the kind to take revenge on a woman."

Cool was torn by indecision. "I only wish I could believe you," he sighed.

It was Marshall Prine who made the choice for him. "It's a risk we'll have to take, I'm afraid, Colonel," he said. "McVey may be telling the truth when he says he had nothing to do with taking Nancy away. After all, you can't lose anything by giving him a chance to take a look across the river. He's worth nothing to you, dead or alive."

Cool was obviously happy that Prine had helped him at an awkward moment. He scowled at Mike. "Mind you, McVey," he warned, "if you're lying you'll be brought to account for it, sooner or later."

"And I want to remind you, Colonel," Mike said, "that I promise nothing, except that I will try. If I don't come back, you'll not need to worry about looking for me. The people over there will have taken care of that. Now, Marsh, tell me exactly what happened. Give it to me quick. I want to be across the river and a considerable distance from this place before daybreak."

"What do you mean — what happened?"

"At the fort when you say Esau tried to kill you."

"The colonel has already told you."

"How did Esau get into the fort and get away with the lady without being seen? How did she get mixed up in it?"

"There had been a wedding rehearsal and there was to be a dance afterward. I went to my room to change. The black man was hiding in my room. He had entered by way of the window which was unlocked. How he got into the fort without being seen I don't know. It was after nightfall, of course. He had a gun in his belt. He told me to draw, and that he was going to kill me. He meant it. Oh, how he meant it. His eyes glared. He had gone insane. It happened that Nancy came to the door about that time. I don't know why, but it probably had to do with some question about the rehearsal or the wedding itself. She heard our voices. As the door was ajar, she opened it. She thought the black man was going to shoot me in cold blood. I believe he meant to do it. She rushed in and stood between us. She pleaded with him not to kill me. She said he'd have to kill her also. He said something about making me suffer as he had suffered. He talked about losing his wife and blamed me for it. Then he slugged me and tied me up with strips from the bedsheet and gagged me so that I damned near suffocated. By the time I really knew where I was again they were gone. It was nearly half an hour before someone came to the room and found me. By that time there was no trace of them. They found a burro under the back stockade wall, by which he must have got in and by which he took Nancy out with him. He must have had a horse somewhere. It was too dark to find tracks."

Prine quit talking. "Anything else?" Mike asked.

"What else could there be?" Prine demanded.

"Why didn't you draw when he challenged you?" Mike asked.

"I was unarmed," Prine snapped. "I told you I had just come from the wedding rehearsal."

"You were running in luck, Marsh," Mike said.

Prine bristled. "Are you insinuating that I would have been afraid to have met that rascal's challenge if I had a pistol on me?"

"Not exactly. I was really thinking that there aren't many women who would think enough of a man to stand in front of him and risk taking a bullet that was meant for him."

He hurried to the corral where he saddled the roan and rigged the pack frame on the best of the two ponies. He rode to his camp and packed what cooking gear, food and bedding he would need.

Prine came for a final word. "There'll be no leniency for this Esau Solomon, no matter what happens," he fumed. "I want that made clear. Nor for you, McVey, if it turns out that you've been lying after all."

"It seems like it ought to be you instead of me that's crossing the river to try to fetch Miss Halstead back, seeing as it was your neck she saved," Mike said.

He rode away then, leaving Prine standing speechless in the darkness. He headed along the river. He could hear the colonel barking orders to the troopers to resume the search. A futile effort. He was sure Esau was across the Missouri. And Nancy Halstead must be there also, either dead or alive.

He had not forgotten that Esau's flatboat was nearby and available for crossing the river, but he ruled against using it. For one thing, the glow of the burning cabin was almost certain to have attracted attention on the hostile side of the Missouri. A man rowing a boat would be an easy target. There would also be the problem of getting the horses safely across. The river was swift and deep at this point. He could not afford to be afoot when he reached the far shore.

He rode back to the ford by which he had crossed with the gold. Dawn was in the sky. The river was higher, and he could see that there would be a considerable stretch of swimming water. The spring rise was beginning. He scanned the shore in the faint light, but found no trace that anyone had crossed here recently. Even the marks of the hoofs of his own mount and the two pack animals that had been made since the last rain were gone. Someone had wiped out all traces of any crossing. To him this meant that the ford had been used, and recently. Dawn-in-the-Sky's body probably had been taken back to Cheyenne country here. There was no way of knowing if Esau had taken Nancy Halstead across at this point also, later on, as a prisoner.

He stripped to the skin, wrapped his garments in his weathered waterproof tarp and lashed the pack as high on the saddle as he could. Gritting his teeth against the chill water, he led the roan and the pack pony into the stream and headed toward the distant shore. When he reached swimming water he clung to the tail of the roan, encouraging both animals by voice and hand.

He could hear the deep rumble of white water not far below the ford. The current was carrying them in that direction, but the roan gamely fought its way ahead, taking both Mike and the pony with it. Even so, Mike began to believe they would not make it when the roan lurched and began to flounder. Its hoofs had found bottom on the west shore. Slipping and sliding, and floundering in deeper holes, he and the two animals made their way over treacherous underfooting, fought through a swampy backwater and finally emerged on dry land.

He found that the tarp had failed to protect his clothes and they were well soaked. His teeth chattering uncontrollably, he got his watertight tin of matches from the pack, gathered dry twigs and built a fire. He spread his clothes on brush where they would catch the heat and crouched over the flame until some of the chill began to leave his bones.

He had rather expected a bullet or an arrow from the brush. He now built the fire higher into a roaring blaze that warmed him faster. He did this deliberately, ignoring the black column of smoke that rose high each time he added fresh fuel to the blaze.

When his blankets had dried, he made a bed within reach of the fire. He heaped heavy driftwood logs on the flames and fed green brush to the coals. He cooked and ate bacon and flapjacks over a smaller separate fire.

He slept for three hours. The sun was midway toward the zenith when he broke camp and saddled. The place where he had spent the early morning was marked by the black column of smoke that still rose from his great fire. No Indian within miles could miss that sight.

His problem was to find one person in that great stretch of plains that lay before him. Two persons. The Great Plains. Buffalo country. Sioux country. Cheyenne country. Hundreds of square miles of it. Bluffs, coulees, wallows. A man could travel for days on it in some areas without seeing a shrub bigger than a switch and not a tree at all. A clump of bunch grass could be miraged in the distance to the size of a hill. What seemed to be bigger hills ahead had a habit of receding tantalizingly as fast as a rider headed toward them, and never could be reached.

In such a vastness he was facing a task akin to finding the proverbial needle in the haystack. There were creeks and rivers in this land, dry at times and raging barriers at others. The Missouri, king of this domain, savage and harsh, slithered back and forth across this mighty expanse. There were labyrinths of eroded bluffs and ravines in which a traveler could lose himself and wander until he starved. There were rattlesnakes. There were the big, savage plains wolves. And the unpredictable grizzly that could kill a buffalo with the stroke of a paw and a man much more easily. Above all, there were the Sioux and the Cheyenne in this land.

Mike had gone deep into this blank space on the map when he had headed for Cheyenne. While that had given him only a sketchy knowledge of the terrain it was at least a help, but he knew that he would never find Esau by his own efforts. There was only one way. Esau must find him, provided Esau wanted to be found. Mike was deliberately letting the tribes know that he was in their hunting grounds. He wanted them also to know why he had come. News of what Esau had done would have traveled through the Indian domain by this time by that mysterious means of communication that was still a mystery to white men.

Young sage hens were plentiful along the way. He killed two with a club and prepared them for his noon meal. He stripped off his shirt and blackened his face and upper body with charcoal from the ashes of the fire. Packing his gear, he saddled and rode into the open. He headed deeper into the rolling plains, leading the pack pony. He rode leisurely. Contrary to the extreme caution with which he had recently traveled over this country while on his way out with his gold, he now made no effort to skirt outcrops or gulches where an enemy might be waiting.

He rode mile after mile, forcing himself to show no sign of doubt, although he was inwardly taut. At times he could almost feel the threat of a bullet or an arrow in his back when he was passing areas where he felt certain eyes were watching him.

The sun grew hot, repaying him for the miseries of the night. He looked neither to the right nor the left. He was sure beyond all doubt, now, that he was being watched — from afar at least, and perhaps from near at hand. There were times when the roan's ears rose and the animal showed uneasiness. It had picked up scent or sound.

He saw antelope bounding away in the distance and be swallowed by the run of the plains. Something had spooked them. A flight of sage hens rose, and the booming of their wings came faintly to him. He marked the faint rise of dust far ahead, and presently crossed a small stream where the tracks of ponies were plain in the dry clay margins.

None of these things were accidental. They were testing him, challenging him in order to make sure they knew his intentions. If he turned back in a panic, they would kill him. And if he continued ahead? That was the gamble.

Noon came and he halted for a meal, again boldly building a large fire that sent smoke high. It was his answer to them, his word that he wanted to be seen. He ate without haste, let the roan and the pony rustle for graze along the small stream by which he had halted, then saddled and resumed the march.

The warmth of the afternoon faded, clouds moved in. In the way of the unpredictable plains weather there probably would be rain soon, perhaps even snow. The land became colorless, merging with the shroudlike hue of the sky. There were no shadows by which to judge the contours of the country, no wind to stir the leafless, brittle vegetation. He swaddled himself in a blanket and the buffalo robe.

The sun was lost and he was not sure in which direction the roan was now carrying him. He no longer trusted his own judgment as to which was north or south and had to depend on the animal. The roan might be circling and heading back, but he doubted it.

Then came the wind, harsh and bullying, like all the qualities of the plains. It buffeted him and the horses. He bent before it in the saddle. The animals bowed their heads and slogged mechanically into it. They pressed deeper and ever deeper into the hunting grounds of the tribes.

He paused to let the animals drink and enjoy surcease from the wind in a huge buffalo wallow where past rains left a clear pool and where the rims were high enough to fend off the rush of weather. The whitening bones of buffalo were thick around the wallow, and Mike saw arrowheads wedged in some so tightly that the effort to remove them would only have shattered them.

Afterward, riding onward, and reaching the crest of one of the great swells in the plain, he sighted live buffalo far to the north — a scattered band of at least a thousand. He suspected this was only a segment of the main herd that Colonel Cool's scouts had reported as the real object of the presence of so many Indians in this area.

The day was dying. Dusk was not far away and he was beginning to lose hope. The wind kept sharpening its teeth. The country became wild and broken with dry washes and boulder-strewn draws in his path. He wrapped his blanket tighter around his bare shoulders, huddling in the saddle against the growing chill. The animals plodded dispiritedly, heads bobbing and sagging.

They advanced down a barren slope of loose rock where the animals slid for yards at a time and leveled off on a flat. Mike found himself confronted by Indians. The wind, moaning through the brush, had covered any sound they might have made in moving out of cover to block his route.

Mike had been hoping for this, using every means to invite it. Even so their appearance startled him. They might have materialized from the cold earth itself. They were Cheyenne. About a dozen of them. They were wrapped in robes and blankets as protection from the wind. Some had repeating rifles jutting from the blankets, others were armed with old Springfields, some of which were muzzle loaders. Several wore ragged, woolen army blouses beneath the blankets, taken, no doubt, from fallen

106

soldiers in the past. The majority preferred the traditional fringed smocks, breeches of elkskin and moccasins.

One, marked by war and responsibility, was a chief. He was Gray Buffalo, father of Dawn-in-the-Sky. Mike had met him in the past when he had acted as interpreter at a powwow between Army generals and tribal leaders. Gray Buffalo's eyes were wise in a powerful face, and implacably fierce. He rode a fine bay horse that bore the Army brand. Some officer must have owned it in the past.

They barred Mike's way. He pulled up, and looked at the chief. "You know me, Gray Buffalo," he said. "I was at the peace talk at Fort Laramie a couple of years ago."

He was sure Gray Buffalo understood the language well enough to get the gist of what he had said, but he repeated it in his sketchy knowledge of the Cheyenne tongue, along with sign language at which he was better versed.

Gray Buffalo made no reply, merely sat gazing at him with that unchanging scorn that he held for the white race. Mike expected to be killed. That was the chance he had taken. Now he was to find out if he had won the gamble.

Then another mounted man came out of

the dusk, pushed through the line of Cheyenne and faced him.

Mike pulled a long breath into his lungs. "Hello, Esau," he said.

He felt now that he would be allowed to live — at least a while longer.

Chapter 6

Esau Solomon had a blanket wrapped around him, and beneath that he wore the smock, leggings and moccasins of a Cheyenne. A rifle was slung at his knee and Mike saw the scabbard of a knife at his belt beneath the blanket.

"Hello, Mike," Esau said. "I see you've changed color. You want to be a nigra too? Or an Injun?"

"It'll wash off," Mike replied. "I became a black man because I figured they'd take me for a friend of yours and wait before lifting my scalp to find out what I had in mind. I knew they'd get word to you that another black man was coming."

"I knew if anyone come it would be you, Mike," Esau said. "An' my people wasn't fooled. Dey knowed you wasn't no black man. They even tol' me it was you. Dey remember you, Mike when you was with de yallalegs. My tribe figgers you as not bein' as bad as the most. Dey know why you quit de Army."

"Your tribe, Esau?"

"I'm Cheyenne now," Esau said. "If I kin

measure up to it. There's things a man has to prove to be a warrior in the tribe. My name from now on is Man-of-the-Night."

"Your name is Esau Solomon," Mike said. "Esau Solomon, who was husband of Ruth. A God-fearing man who read Scriptures and abided by the Commandments."

"There's things that kain't be washted off like you'll be able to wash the black off you," Esau said. "Such as blood on de hands. De blood o' my wife."

"There's no blood on anyone's hands," Mike said. "You know that, Esau. Nobody knows whether Marsh Prine could have helped Ruth. Only God knows."

Esau's stony expression did not change. Mike said, "I came for the young lady. I came to take her back to Flagg."

Esau's features became harder. "Why didn't her man come to git her?" he demanded. "Did he send you in his place, Mike?"

"I didn't come here on account of Marsh Prine," Mike said. "I'm here because of you, Esau, and the young lady. Marsh Prine means nothing to me. But you do. You're my friend. I would not be alive if it hadn't been for you."

Esau's expression still remained harsh. "You know what will happen to you if they catch you," Mike went on. "Kidnaping is a hanging offense. Cool is threatening things even worse. You know what you could be in for."

"I know."

"And I know you. The young lady hasn't been harmed. I'll take her back with me. That will be one load off your conscience, at least. You made a mistake. It can be corrected."

He was closely watching Esau's eyes as he spoke. He was trying to determine whether Nancy Halstead was still alive or whether the Indians had taken vengeance on her. Then he began to breathe easier. Something in Esau's expression told him that he was speaking of a living person. Nancy Halstead was still a captive.

"De only one what must come for her is dat man," Esau said.

"Prine? You still want to kill him, Esau?"

Esau's features remained unyielding. "Vengeance is mine, saith the Lord," Mike said. "You've read that in the Book."

"De Book say other things too. An eye for an eye, a tooth for a tooth."

"You had your chance to kill Prine back at the fort," Mike said. "Why didn't you do it then? But you stole the girl he was to marry. Why?"

"She stood in front of him," Esau said. "She would have took the bullet herself. It was him dat was guilty, not her."

"The truth is that you couldn't bring yourself to kill him in cold blood," Mike said.

"Dat man wouldn't defend hisself," Esau said. "His pistol was hangin' on de wall in a holster. I laid my gun near it on a stand. I tol' him we'd race fer it an' shoot it out. He wouldn't move. Den I tol' him we'd fight with our bare hands to death. He wouldn't move. De young lady begged me not to kill him. She wouldn't stand out of de way. I decided that if'n I took her with me he'd be man enough to come after me to try to git her back. So I slugged him an' tied him up, an' left with de young lady."

"How did you manage that? Didn't she scream or resist?"

"She promised she wouldn't if I'd let dat man live. We crawled out by de way I got in. I'd dug a hole under de stockade. Dey had only one sentry on dat side an' it was easy to git in an' out. One of de Cheyenne was waitin' fer me at the river with de canoe in which we'd come across. We had ponies waitin' on this side."

Darkness was at hand. A chill, misty rain was setting in. The Cheyenne had sat motionless during the conversation. Now Gray Buffalo spoke sharply in Cheyenne and the ponies were stirred into motion.

"Come," Esau said, motioning to Mike.

The Cheyenne moved in and Mike found himself surrounded. "Where?" he asked.

"To de village," Esau answered.

"Am I a prisoner?"

Esau didn't answer at once. "Dat remains to be seen," he finally said.

Gray Buffalo lifted Mike's rifle, pistol and knife from him. He rode, hemmed in, through the rain and gathering darkness down a long draw between rock-studded bluffs. Rounding a bend, he saw ahead an encampment of a dozen or so lodges, scattered along a small stream. The lodges loomed like great jack-o'-lanterns in the deepening darkness, for their walls of scraped buffalo hide were translucent, and glowed with the cheerful ruddiness of the cook-fires that burned within. The fragrance of buffalo meat and other food that was being prepared came on the wind.

Young braves came shouting and running to meet them and the braves took care of the ponies as the warriors swung down. Esau touched Mike's arm. "Dis way," he said.

Gray Buffalo led them to the biggest lodge which stood at the center of the village. He held back the buffalo robe that acted as a curtain over the entrance and motioned Mike to enter.

Mike had been in Indian lodges many times. Many of them were odorous places, not too clean and infested with insects. This Cheyenne home was much larger than the average and it was clean, neat and made comfortable with pelts underfoot and on the pallets. Buffalo meat was broiling on a spit and an iron pot steamed with stew.

A Cheyenne woman was tending the food, but she did not turn toward him. Such curiosity would not have been polite in an Indian wife. She was Elk Woman. Dawn-in-the-Sky's young sister, in a finely tanned beaded smock, was helping her mother.

Nancy Halstead sat on a pallet of robes and blankets at the rear of the lodge. Her eyes were lackluster, her face thin and colorless. Her lips were tight set. She still wore a bedraggled dress that she must have donned for the wedding rehearsal. It had been a flowery affair with a wide skirt over several petticoats, and trimmed with lace. Now it was a limp, soiled ruin. Her slippers were missing. A pair of moccasins that must have belonged to the young Cheyenne girl lay near the pallet, evidently refused by Nancy Halstead. Her feet were bare. She was trembling, but not from the outer chill, for the lodge was very warm in contrast to the cold rain that drummed on the walls. Occasional drops found their way through the smoke wings and hissed in the fire or spattered in the cookpot.

Nancy Halstead's head lifted a trifle. She stared dully at the arrivals. Then her chin sank again. Mike discovered something that horrified him. Her waxen hands were clutched on the handle of a knife that had a thin and wicked six-inch blade.

Mike found his voice. "Miss Halstead!"

Her head lifted again. She studied him and he had never seen such stark despair, such lost hope in human eyes. Into those eyes came the glitter of desperate decision. Her two hands lifted the knife and held it poised, ready to plunge it into her heart.

"No!" Mike exclaimed desperately, "No! I'm Mike McVey!"

She paused but continued to gaze at him in that terrible way as though she had heard but was determined not to be deluded or swerved from her purpose. It was as though her mind was far, far away, already occupied with the mystery of death. Here was a person who had given herself up as no longer living.

Mike dropped the blanket. Then he remembered the blacking on his skin. He realized that to this refined girl who had found herself suddenly carried back to the Stone Age he was only another savage.

"I'm Mike McVey," he repeated. "The man you laughed at when he was thrown from his horse that night you arrived on the steamboat at the Fort Flagg landing. I'm the man you talked Colonel Cool into releasing from the guardhouse after I had that brawl with the steamboat captain."

"Steamboat captain? Thrown from horse?"

She was repeating the phrases like a child in a dream.

"I'm the man you talked to at Esau Solomon's place the day you came there to find out what had happened to Esau's wife," Mike went on. He was talking quietly, but very earnestly, trying to break through the apathy and reach her mind, bring her back to reality. He had to talk her into lowering the knife from her breast.

Behind him he heard Esau murmuring a prayer, pleading that Nancy Halstead would not use the knife on herself. Mike continued to talk, "I came to help you. I blacked myself so the Cheyenne would know I was a friend of Esau's and would let me come into their country to find him."

A new light came slowly into her eyes. She

studied him very carefully, very cautiously. It was evident she was attempting to decide if he was trying to deceive her. At least she was beginning to think and reason — sanely.

Slowly the dullness faded from her eyes. He saw a hint of color come into her throat which had been the hue of slate. It moved into her haggard face. "What did you say your name is?" she asked.

Mike repeated his name, repeated what he had said about his meetings with her. She peered closer. Mike chanced moving a pace toward her. At once her grip tightened on the knife and the desperation raced back into her eyes. He halted. He could still hear Esau murmuring the prayer. Elk Woman and the chief and their daughter were somewhere in the lodge, but he did not turn to look at them. He knew that, like Esau, they were standing frozen, aware that a wrong word would be fatal.

Mike ran his hands hard over his face, rubbing away some of the blackness. "There's no need for the knife," he said. "Nobody is going to harm you here. If that had been in their minds it would already have been done. I came to find you. I promised Colonel Cool and Marshall Prine that I'd try. And here I am."

The young Cheyenne girl spoke. Her name was Snow Dove, and, like Dawn-in-the-Sky, she had been taught English at a missionary school in the days before the bitter plains warfare had broken out. "McVey, he tell the truth. We know him. He is white of skin, not black like Man-of-the-Night. He speaks the truth. My people would have killed anyone else, but it was Man-of-the-Night's wish that he be allowed to come here and speak to you."

Nancy Halstead studied Mike's face, seeking out the truth. Then she lowered the knife a trifle.

"You do remember me now, don't you?" Mike asked.

She nodded. "Yes. I remember you. I remember you falling from the horse. And the fight. I thought you were an Indian."

"I know why you were brought here," Mike said. "I know what happened that night at the fort when Esau Solomon came there. Stop thinking of death. You will live. Have you been harmed?"

"Harmed?" She tried to recollect. "If expecting to be killed every minute is harm, then I've been harmed. If being stoned by children and the squaws is harm, then I've been harmed."

"Where did you get that knife?"

"I snatched it out of Elk Woman's hand yesterday when she got careless."

"You've had it all this time?"

"Yes."

"Why did you wait until now to decide to use it on yourself?"

"I've felt from the first that the black man means to kill me. And I know why he's waited."

"Why?"

"He wants to kill Marshall Prine. He blames him for the death of his wife. He came to the fort to kill Marsh, but I happened to be able to interfere. He tried to force Marsh into a duel with guns, then into a hand-to-hand fight. When that didn't work he took me with him. I know why he's kept me alive. He expected Marsh to try to find me. Then he'd kill him."

She was telling the truth. Neither Mike nor Esau had any answer for that. "He hates me," she went on. "Like he hates Marsh Prine."

"I don' hate you, lady," Esau said. "You don't understand." He spoke to Mike. "She won't eat. Ain't et a thing since I brung her here."

"You'll eat something now, won't you?" Mike asked her. He spoke to Snow Dove. "Bring her some food, little sister."

119

The Cheyenne girl moved to the fire with a wooden platter on which she placed meat and stew. She brought them to Nancy Halstead along with a hornspoon.

Nancy Halstead hesitated a long time. She finally looked to Mike for advice. "I don't want to die," she admitted. "I want to live as much as any person."

She added, "I trust you, McVey." She accepted the platter. She tested the food gingerly at first, her tongue and throat refusing for a time to accept it. The girl brought a horn of water and she drank. Then she tried the food again. Slowly at first, then with a fierce, healthy appetite.

Mike watched a transformation. The decision to die faded from Nancy Halstead's wan face. The color became stronger, some of the waxen resignation seemed to go with each passing moment. It was replaced by the glow of life, the love of existence. His own throat became tight with the wonder and glory of it. He looked at Esau. In the black man's expression was some of that same wonder, along with thankfulness, as though grateful that a prayer had been answered.

Esau motioned him to follow, and turned to leave the lodge. Mike did not move. Esau halted and understood. "She'll be all right now," he said gruffly. "Snow Dove and Elk Woman will look after her."

Mike moved to Nancy Halstead. "Let me have the knife," he said gently.

She paused eating and sat considering it for a long time. Then she drew the knife from where she had hidden it in the folds of her dress and handed it to him. "You came here to take me back," she said. "You told me that. You promised me that."

"That's right," Mike said. "We'll start in the morning." He looked at the others. At Esau. At Elk Woman. At Gray Buffalo. Before Mike knew his intention Gray Buffalo snatched from his hand the knife Nancy Halstead had just surrendered to him.

His gaze met the eyes of the white girl. The hope that had flamed in her was suddenly gone. They both knew that they would not be allowed to leave this village tomorrow to head back to Fort Flagg. Not tomorrow. Perhaps never. They both were prisoners now.

Mike followed Esau from the big lodge to a smaller one where a surly squaw, who was fat and wrinkled, with cruel eyes, was cooking meat on a spit over the fire. At Esau's curt command she dished up food to both himself and Mike, which they ate with their fingers, no utensils being provided. A warrior with a crooked nose and a deep scar on his cheek joined the squaw and ate apart from Esau and Mike. The warrior had a rifle at his side. He favored Mike with one baleful glance then ignored him and Esau. It was plain that Mike at least was a prisoner and under guard.

"My razor and soap were in my camp pack," Mike said to Esau. "Along with some clean underwear. I'm in need of a shave and a bath. Can do?"

Esau left and presently returned with Mike's bedroll and warsack. Also his saddle. He sat the saddle in the lodge and handed the warsack over. He talked sharply to the squaw in Cheyenne. She answered shrilly, objecting to his request. Mike heard Esau mention Gray Buffalo's Cheyenne name. That subdued the squaw. She ungraciously slammed out of the lodge and presently returned with an object that caused Mike's brows to arch. It was a metal bathtub just large enough for a person to immerge. Another relic of some raid on an Army outfit.

The squaw brought water and poured it into the tub. It was fresh from the stream and icy cold. Mike stood waiting. Esau, the squaw and the warrior kept staring woodenly at him — also waiting.

"No hot water?" Mike asked.

Esau's teeth showed in a grin. "Don't tell me you've gone dat soft, Mike."

"I've waited months for a hot bath," Mike said. "I could hope, couldn't I?"

"I'm goin' to enjoy dis," Esau said. "At dat, Mike, you got to admit it's better dan de crick where I have to wash."

Mike tested the water with his fingers and winced. "Get out of here!" he barked at the squaw.

The Cheyenne woman understood. She uttered a cackle of derisive laughter and planted herself firmly on a blanket with the intention of remaining.

"She's goin' to enjoy it too," Esau said. "Be happy, Mike. She had a club ready which she aimed to use on you mighty hard. Dat's de way she likes to handle prisoners. I talked her out o' it."

"Thanks," Mike said, resignedly fingering the water. "Maybe I'd be better off dead. Do you think you could at least influence her into rounding up a little hot water for shaving. These whiskers of mine don't give in easy in cold water."

After much shrill and angry argument with Esau, during which the squaw gave Mike many scornful glances, a battered tin basin was produced in which water was quickly heated over the coals of the fire.

Mike shaved, with the squaw looking on and making comments in Cheyenne that he did not entirely understand, but which he knew were far from complimentary. When he was finished scraping away his growth of beard, she clapped her hands over her mouth in mock amazement at the transformation.

Mike again ordered her to leave, but she only jeered him. So he stripped and bathed in the icy water, chattering and tingling. He managed to scrub off most of the soot. The squaw again pretended to be amazed at the change. "He white man!" she screeched in English. "He pale man! Not black, not brown!" She danced around him, pretending awe and worship.

Mike tried to ignore her. He got from his pack his spare socks and underwear and dressed. He started to leave the lodge, but Esau blocked his path.

"Where you goin', Mike?"

"Back to the Halstead girl," Mike said.

"You an' me are to put up here in this lodge," Esau said.

"I see. Are you supposed to see to it that I don't try to get away?"

"I reckon not, Mike. I don' think they trust me that far yet. You better git a night's rest. You goin' to need it. An' so am I. We're breakin' camp in de mornin'."

"Where are we going?"

"I got no idea, Mike."

And that was the way it was. At daybreak he was awakened by a stir of activity. The squaw was hurrying about, gathering the meager cooking and camping effects, packing them in parfleche bags. Without ceremony she began dismantling the lodge itself almost over the heads of Mike and Esau who finished dressing hurriedly and scrambled out into the drizzling rain.

Bony ponies equipped with pack saddles and slings for travois poles were being brought up. The entire village was being dismantled. Lodgepoles were being dropped and some of them used as travois poles on which belongings were lashed. Warriors squatted stoically in the rain under blankets and ponchos like disconsolate owls, letting the women do all the work.

Mike walked to where Gray Buffalo's lodge was being dismantled. Only the poles stood. Elk Woman and Snow Dove had stripped away the buffalo hide covering, unlaced the sections and rolled them into bundles to be placed on the travois. They worked stolidly, but swiftly, without wasted motion.

Nancy Halstead stood wrapped in a buffalo robe, watching helplessly. Elk Woman screamed an impatient order at her, snatched the robe from her and gave her a push. Confusedly, she tried to help with felling the ribs of the lodge. Her inexperienced, cold-numbed hands were unequal to the task. Elk Woman pushed her aside and she and the young Cheyenne girl dropped and bound the poles into the three travois frames that were needed to carry a chief's effects. Pack saddles were piled with additional bundles.

"Good morning," Mike said to Nancy Halstead. "That's only a manner of speaking, of course. I've seen better weather."

She didn't recognize him for a moment and instinctively shrank from him. Then she realized who he was. Her gaze traveled over him. "You've changed," she said.

"I'm not sure it's for the better," he said. "My hotel last night seemed to lack mirrors and was mighty short on hot water. I tried to return to my natural color. I hope the effort was worth while. Just what color am I this morning?"

"Sort of a sooty gray," she said, and even tried to smile. It was a failure. "Where are we going?"

"I don't know," Mike said. "Neither does Esau."

Esau came up to them. "You'll stay with

Gray Buffalo's lodge, missy," he told the girl. "Do what Elk Woman an' Snow Dove tell you to do. If'n you don', Elk Woman will beat you. Don' blame her. She still grievin' fer my Ruth. An' don' try to git away. All de squaws air jest waitin' an excuse to club you if'n you try anythin' foolish."

"What if we just set out for Fort Flagg?" Mike asked.

Esau shook his head. "Don' try it. Dey'll kill the both o' you. Dey'd have killed you before this, 'cept I talked dem out of it because you was my friend. Dey know you stood up fer the treaty ag'in Colonel Cool, but you's a white man an' dey can't fergit dat."

Esau was all Indian. He turned and walked to where the straggling group of Cheyenne men sat and squatted down on the outer fringe among the young braves. He pulled a blanket over his head and merged with their silent ranks.

Mike found Nancy Halstead gazing at him with tormented eyes. "I'm sorry," she said.

"Sorry? You mean for me?"

"Yes. I'm the cause of getting you into this terrible thing."

"Now hold on. It isn't that way at all. It —"

"Esau had told me about you before you were brought to the village last night. He told me that if anyone tried to find me in Indian country it would be you. Now why did he know that?"

"I haven't the faintest idea," Mike said. "A hunch, I suppose."

"Surely they must be only trying to frighten us. They can't really mean to keep us with them, to kill us if we try to leave."

"They mean it," Mike said.

"But why? You've been their friend. They know that. The black man told me so. Why would they want to kill you?"

"They don't unless I force it on them by trying to pull out."

"I see. They know you'd go back to the fort and put the troops on them."

"That might be the reason. It's a good one."

She eyed him. "What other reason could there be?"

"I'm not sure."

"What do you mean you're not sure."

"I'm wondering why Gray Buffalo is wandering around in such weather with only a few lodges and a handful of warriors. He's no small potatoes as a chief. He's a big man among the Cheyenne. A war chief who can talk with the great ones. He was chief of a

128

village of more than a hundred lodges not so long in the past."

"I don't follow you," she said. "Is it out of the ordinary?"

"Usually it would be called loss of face or prestige," Mike said. "Somehow I can't believe that. There are several other things about this setup that bother me. It's been a hard winter. These people ought to be making meat and storing up new buffalo robes before the animals shed. I sighted a big bunch of buffalo off the north yesterday. This village is eating fresh meat, but there's only enough to keep them going. This isn't a hunting camp. They're killing only what they need for each day, so as not to be burdened with any extra weight. That means they either aim to travel a long way, or be able to move fast if needed."

"That means they're going to take me — us — farther from Fort Flagg, farther from help, doesn't it?" she said.

"It looks that way. But there are other things I don't understand. This is really a war party, even though there are squaws along. Nearly all these Cheyenne women are tough, mature squaws who know their business. They know how to campaign and move fast, and put up with hardships. The same with the men. There are about twenty of them, which is a lot more than there should be in a camp of a dozen lodges. They're warriors, experienced fighting men. Picked men. There isn't a young child in camp. Only a few boys who are strong enough to keep up, and a few young braves. No babies at all. No girls. Snow Dove is about the youngest girl in camp, and she's far from being a child."

"What do you make of it? What are you trying to say?"

"I wish I knew," Mike admitted.

Elk Woman came hurrying and roughly seized Nancy Halstead by the arm, and hurried her away, breaking up the conversation. Nancy was ordered to carry the heavy bundles to where Snow Dove was loading the travois.

Nancy tried to give Mike a smile as she struggled past with a burden. "It seems that I've got to earn my board and keep," she said to him. "How about you?"

"I'd lose face if I did squaw work," Mike said. "I might try beating you with a club if you don't move fast enough. That's a man's job in the scheme of things here."

"Don't the men ever do any work?" she asked the next time she toiled past. She gave the silent group of blanketed warriors a scornful glare.

"Careful!" Mike said. "Don't try to upset a system that is very satisfactory as far as they're concerned. They hunt and make war."

"They look like a pack of lazy good-for-nothings to me," she sniffed. "I take it the system is successful from your point of view also?"

"It has its good points," Mike said.

This time her smile had more life. The past few hours had worked wonders. The waxen, haggard apathy was gone, replaced by return of her natural lilting spirit.

"Keep it up," Mike said when his next chance came to speak to her.

"Keep what up?"

"Your spunk."

"I'm trying," she said. "I sort of ran low on it for a while, didn't I?"

"That's all over with, isn't it?"

She knew what he meant. "Yes, I think so."

"You've got to be sure. But you're not. Why?"

She looked at him levelly. "You've heard that old saying about there being a fate worse than death. I can't ever become an Indian. Not like Esau Solomon is trying to be. And I don't think he ever will either. Completely that is."

"You mean —"

"Elk Woman told me that I am to be married to a Cheyenne warrior. It seems the arrangements have already been made but the event evidently isn't to take place immediately. My guess is that it is being delayed for some reason."

Elk Woman came rushing up to halt the conversation. She had a stout stick in her hand, which she lifted overhead to deliver a vicious blow at Nancy. The stick would have struck its victim in the face. Mike moved in, parried the blow with an arm and tore the stick from the squaw's hands.

Elk Woman began screeching wildly in Cheyenne. Several warriors came running. One was brandishing a hatchet. He hurled the weapon with all his force when still a dozen strides away. Mike ducked the flying blade. Another Cheyenne aimed a rifle pointblank at him and squeezed the trigger — a second too late to kill him, for Esau arrived and batted the muzzle upward in time.

Gray Buffalo came shouldering into the foreground, barking harsh words in the Cheyenne tongue. That quieted the warriors. They lowered their weapons. The blood lust faded out of them slowly. In their unpredictable way, some began to grin, seeing Mike's narrow escape as very humorous. They turned and walked away, with Gray Buffalo also stalking away, leaving Mike and Esau standing there.

"You'll never come closer to it, Mike," Esau said. "Next time, I don't figger I could hold dem."

Mike stood for a time, frowning, thinking. "It wasn't you that stopped them, Esau," he finally said. "It was Gray Buffalo. Why? He doesn't really give a hoot whether I'm alive or dead."

"I reckon dat's right," Esau admitted. "Why should he?"

"But he wants me alive. He said something to the warriors that I didn't quite get the gist, but whatever it was it cooled them down. What's in his mind?"

"I wouldn't know," Esau said. "But somethin's goin' on. I can't figger out what it is."

"You saved my bacon when you batted that rifle into the air, Esau," Mike said. "I'd have been dead no matter whether Gray Buffalo wanted it that way or not. That's another score I owe you."

He extended a hand to shake. Esau refused it, but made the Indian gesture of friendship, then turned and walked away.

Mike walked to where Elk Woman was bullying Nancy Halstead at the camp work. "You would have had the warriors kill me with your screaming, Mother," he said. "Is this the thanks you give me for trying to bring the yellowleg medicine man to help Dawn-in-the-Sky?"

"But he did not come," Elk Woman said in English. "My daughter is dead. This white woman cannot take her place, but I will see to it that she works like a dog."

"She had nothing to do with it," Mike said. "You must not take it out on her. You are wrong. She is a good, pure woman. She came from far away to marry the yellowleg medicine man, but that does not mean she can be blamed for what he might have done."

Elk Woman spat in contempt. She spoke viciously to Nancy in Cheyenne. Nancy did not understand the words which Mike knew were an order to work harder at the packing. Elk Woman tried to seize her by the hair in order to punish her. Instead, Nancy caught the squaw's arms and threw her sprawling off her feet. It was a case of being taken by surprise rather than of superior strength. But it had its effect.

Elk Woman got to her feet. She was far stronger, far tougher and experienced in the hair-pulling, vicious combats with other squaws that were a part of their life. Something in Nancy's attitude gave her pause.

Nancy stood grimly determined to defend herself — to the death if need be. Mike saw that in her eyes and Elk Woman saw it too. Typical of the Indian nature, the Cheyenne woman dropped the matter and hurried away to continue her duties, leaving Nancy to her own devices.

Nancy resumed her menial task. Snow Dove, who had copied her mother's hostile attitude, changed also and became more tolerant toward the captive. She attempted to maintain a superior attitude toward the novice, but it was obvious she was impressed and a little awed that anyone would physically challenge Elk Woman's wrath.

Finally, the village was ready to move out. Gray Buffalo mounted the pad saddle of his big bay horse. Esau appeared, leading Mike's saddled roan and the pack pony.

"You are lucky," Esau said. "You're to ride. Most prisoners would have walked with the horses an' squaws."

The other warriors mounted. The young braves began whooping and chirping as they rounded up the remuda and shoved them abreast of the line of march. The squaws prodded and screeched the beasts of burden into motion. Travois poles creaked and left twin tracks in the rain-softened earth. The rain hissed in the embers of the deserted cookfires which stood in the dryer circles where the lodges had been. Gray Buffalo and his people were making no attempt to hide the evidence that they had camped here, nor were they concerned about the trail they were now leaving.

Two warriors on ponies sat looking at Esau and Mike and Nancy, who had not joined the moving procession. "All right, Mike," Esau said. "Better mount up."

"What about Miss Halstead?" Mike asked.

"She'll walk with de other squaws."

Mike turned and lifted the girl in his arms, intending to swing her onto the saddle of the roan. He was forced to halt, for the two Cheyenne had moved in and thrust the crossed barrels of their rifles in his way.

He sat Nancy Halstead back on her feet. "We'll both walk," he said.

"That isn't necessary," she said. "Don't try to be so gallant. I'm not made of sugar and spice. I'll show Elk Woman I can keep up as long as any Cheyenne woman. You'll only antagonize them again."

She was now wearing the moccasins she had previously refused. One of the squaws had possession of the satin slippers that had been part of her costume and was determinedly clumping along on the broken high heels. Nancy had a blanket wrapped around her and had done her hair in a plait that hung down her back. It came to Mike suddenly that here was an invincible spirit, an unbreakable will.

"Marsh Prine is a lucky man," he said abruptly.

She eyed him questioningly. "Lucky? You mean because Esau Solomon didn't kill him? You're right, of course."

"I was thinking of something else," he said.

The two warriors parted them then, forcing her to join the squaws and work ponies. Mike marched alone, leading the roan, refusing to mount. Esau rode for a time with the two warriors who had evidently been appointed as guards over Mike. Mike appreciated the black man's presence. He knew Esau was staying with him to make sure his guards did not take it in mind to become bored with their task and kill the captive.

The rain came harder and slanted drearily into their faces on the teeth of a biting wind. They marched all day, with only short pauses for food and to rest the stock. Mike could only guess at the direction they were heading, for all landmarks were hidden under the gloomy sky.

They camped well before dark. The rain had tapered off. The squaws did not bother to pitch the lodges. The Cheyenne chewed on jerky or cold leftovers from the cookpots and settled down under robes and blankets and were instantly asleep.

Mike got the last of his pemmican and smoked tongue from his warsack and shared it with Esau and Nancy. Esau cut thin slices of the pemmican with his knife and passed them around.

"What is this nasty stuff?" Nancy asked ruefully after testing the offering. "Are we down to eating shoe leather?"

"Chaw hard," Mike said. "It's pemmican. Made it myself from the recipe of an old Crow woman. It's the best you'll get — and the cleanest in camp."

She huddled between him and Esau and followed his example by laboring on the cold, hard fare with a healthy appetite.

Gray Buffalo loomed suddenly out of the rain. He spat something scornfully in the Cheyenne tongue, then snatched the remains of the food from Esau's hand and hurled it contemptuously away. He did not even glance at Mike and Nancy who sat frozen with astonishment, their food still poised. They expected the same treatment, but it did not come.

Gray Buffalo grunted a command. Esau obeyed, getting hastily to his feet. Gray Buffalo snatched from his shoulders the buffalo robe that had protected him from the cold, leaving him bare to the waist to face the weather. The chief berated him fiercely for a moment in the native tongue, then strode away.

"What is it?" Nancy breathed, frightened.

Mike did not answer for a time. He waited. Esau moved away from them, apart from the warriors and stood alone, and remained there.

"What is this all about?" Nancy asked again. "Why is he standing there? He'll freeze."

"There's nothing you can do about it. He won't freeze — we hope. It isn't that cold. And if it goes that way, then he'll freeze."

"I don't understand. What are they doing to him? Is this some kind of punishment for bringing us into the village? Some kind of torture?"

"You could call it that. It's what they call a test. What white men call an initiation. It'll get worse before it's over, I'm afraid."

"Worse?"

"Esau is joining the tribe, becoming a full-fledged Cheyenne warrior. There are certain things a Cheyenne has to do, things he has to prove, before he can be accepted as a member, especially as a warrior."

139

"Then it *is* torture! How awful! Can we help him?"

"Good God, no! That would be the last thing in the world Esau would want. He'd be disgraced, laughed at as the man who needed the help of a squaw. Stay away from him. Don't even look at him. Above all, don't show pity for him. If you must do something, taunt him, throw stones at him, jab sticks into him, beat him with a switch. Try to weaken him, make him beg. The other squaws will do those things. This is your chance to pay him off for what he did."

"But I don't want to pay him off."

Mike peered close at her. "He's the man who brought you into this, remember? Don't you hold that against him? Don't you want to see him punished?"

"He was out of his mind that night," she said. "He kept telling me how much he had loved the Cheyenne girl who died. He wanted to kill Marsh Prine that night, but I doubt if he does any longer. He told me he had no hatred of me and that he was sorry to have to take me. No, I no longer want to see him punished. I pity him. He loved her so much. So very, very much. All he's trying to do now is forget. He'll never really be a Cheyenne, no matter what he goes through

140

to try to prove it. He'll always be what he was — Esau Solomon, a gentle man who wanted to live in peace."

"I doubt if Marsh Prine will look at it that way," Mike said. "Nor Roscoe Cool."

"I'm afraid you're right," she said.

"And Esau may change," Mike warned. "The tests he's in for are the kind to mark the soul of a man, if he goes all the way to becoming a warrior."

"Do you want to tell me about it?"

"No," Mike said. "And, above all, reconcile yourself to it. We can't do anything about it. Get some sleep now."

He arranged a headrest for her and added his blanket to the robe she had covered herself with. He rolled up in his own bedding and pulled the tarp over both of them to ward off the rain.

The damp chill of the night made real sleep impossible. At times Mike dropped into dream-torn slumber, only to drift back to awareness of his discomfort. Each time he opened his eyes, he saw the black, silent figure standing in the darkness, enduring the brunt of the cold. Esau was meeting his first test.

Mike was aware that Nancy looked at Esau also, each time she aroused. He heard her sighing in pity for the black man. She instinctively huddled closer to Mike for protection from the terrors of this camp and this night. He drew her blanketed form close against him, an arm around her to further comfort her.

Chapter 7

The rain ended during the night. In the way of the plains, a balmy wind moved in before daybreak, and the day promised to be clear and warm for a change.

Mike and Nancy were awakened by the shrill laughter and jeering of the squaws. They were tormenting Esau. He still stood apart, as immobile as a statue, paying no attention to them and their antics. A squaw came from the stream with a parfleche filled with icy water and poured it over him. Another began tormenting his face with the stiff branches of a bush. He did not flinch nor look at them. He was struck with clubs and stones. A woman rushed up with a stick which she began jabbing into his ribs. Screeching with glee, she danced around him, darting the pointed implement at his face, so dangerously close it seemed an eye would be pierced at any moment. Esau did not even blink.

"Stop them!" Nancy moaned. "Stop them! How cruel can they be?" She would have interfered, but Mike held her back.

It ended abruptly. Gray Buffalo gave an

order and the squaws halted their punishment, hastening to turn their attention to breaking camp.

Bruises showed on Esau's face where some of the stones had struck. Blood streaked his body. He moved a stiff step, halted, and Mike could see him forcing himself by an effort of will to take a second step. He had stood for so many hours in one position his muscles were numbed.

"You *must* help him!" Nancy whispered.

"No," Mike answered.

Esau steadied, took another step and another. Then he began to come to life. He had made it, passed the new test. His great body had met the challenge of the night and had conquered. The injuries the squaws had inflicted were nothing compared to that triumph.

Elk Woman came with a switch, threatening to use it on Nancy for dallying. Nancy laughed at her. "Cheyenne woman!" she said. "If you ever touch me with a stick again, I'll tear your hair out and feed it to the birds to make nests."

She walked away to help Snow Dove with the packing. Elk Woman stood, a hand clapped over her mouth to prevent the entrance of an evil spirit during such a display of surprise.

"Looks like you've got a wildcat on your hands, Mother," Mike said. "With claws sharper than your own."

Elk Woman, subdued, hurried to oversee the final packing of the travois. She rehitched the knots Nancy's untrained fingers had formed and demonstrated the proper way — this time without scolding or blows.

Mike saw that Snow Dove, at the stream, was tending Esau's bruises and cuts with cold water and Indian remedies — a ministration he was enduring with a warrior's stoical indifference.

Nancy walked again with the squaws and pack animals. Mike also walked, trying to win his point that the white woman captive should be mounted — and failing. The two warrior guards followed him as before, with Esau hovering near on an Indian pony.

"Where are we heading?" Mike asked Esau.

He did not answer, merely riding straight ahead, his eyes fixed on the horizon. Mike had forgotten that a man submitting himself to the code that must be endured to win a warrior's feather, was not only forbidden to show pain, affection or any other emotion, he could not even speak until he was accepted or had failed to meet the bitter requirements.

The other Cheyenne relaxed as the sun warmed them and the young braves became playful. Mike was their target. When they believed they were catching him off-guard, they would hurl their ponies into a gallop and bear down on him suddenly, screeching and brandishing a lance or with an arrow nocked to the string of a bent bow.

At close range they would let fly. They never aimed to kill him, only to test his nerves. If he had panicked and attempted to dodge, he likely would have taken one of the missiles. But, each time, he walked steadily ahead without swerving, looking straight through the fierce, mocking faces of his tormenters as though they did not exist. He was as stoical in this test as had been Esau when the squaws had badgered him.

Finally a lance tore from his shoulders the blanket he had folded and slung there. He stooped and picked up both blanket and the lance. For the first time, he mounted the roan and prodded it into a run.

The young Cheyenne who owned the lance had halted his pony and was wheeling it intending to return and retrieve his weapon. Mike was upon him before he realized what was coming. Mike did not use the lethal end of the spear. He drove the hardwood butt into the Cheyenne's stomach, hurling the startled brave from his pony. The victim turned a somersault on the muddy ground and lay there, doubled, wheezing for breath.

The other Indians, always quick to demean and humiliate even one of their own, began howling with laughter and pointing in derision. The fallen Cheyenne finally got to his feet, still green around the lips. His pony had stampeded out of his reach. Its mud-caked owner was forced to endure more taunting and laughter as he labored on foot to round up the animal. He finally succeeded after much running and coaxing.

Mike slid to the ground and resumed his way on foot, leading the roan and his pack pony. That ended the baiting.

The march continued. Nancy spoke to Mike later when the procession had halted at a stream. "How long are they going to keep this up?"

Mike saw that she was weary. Some of the fears had returned. "I'm sorry," she added. "I'm not an Indian — yet. I don't want to show any weakness in front of them, but I wonder how long I can keep this up."

Mike waited until the village resumed the march. He walked to where Nancy trudged along with the squaws, took her by the arm, and led her to where the roan stood. He lifted her off her feet and did what the two Cheyenne guards had prevented him from doing on the other occasion. He swung her into the saddle. They made an irresolute move to interfere, then gave it up.

"I'm beginning to believe you'd make a good Cheyenne warrior yourself," Nancy said as he shortened the stirrups. "They must think so too, for they're beginning to respect you, especially since the way you manhandled that vicious young devil with the lance."

"That seems to go double for you," Mike said. "I've noticed that Elk Woman is more friendly to you, and that she's forgotten about using a switch on you. And some of these young Cheyenne are looking you over from a new viewpoint, figuring how many ponies you're worth. There's competition for your hand."

She shuddered a little, then colored. "Such crude talk!" she sniffed. "I feel guilty, taking your horse. You've walked as far as I have."

"I'm a little more broke in to it, and not on a ballroom floor or promenading around at tea parties," Mike said.

"That's not very kind," she said. She added, "Even if it is true."

"I don't think it'll last much longer anyway," Mike said. "We seem to be reaching our destination."

He pointed ahead. At first she didn't know what she was supposed to be seeing. "It's that haze above the horizon," he explained. "It's smoke."

"Smoke? A prairie fire? I've heard of such things."

"It's no prairie fire. Who ever heard of a prairie fire at this time of year after all this rain? Don't they teach you anything at tea parties? That's from a lot of fires. I'd say there's a big Indian camp somewhere ahead. That's where we're going, I reckon."

But he was wrong. Gray Buffalo ordered them to camp at that moment. This time the lodges were set up. The chief and the older warriors rode away, vanishing in the direction of the haze on the horizon. They did not return until after dark.

When morning came the camp was broken, but in a leisurely manner in contrast to the hectic mornings of the past. There was an air of expectant excitement among the Cheyenne. Furthermore they were decked out in their best. The warriors wore fine elkskin vests, beaded chaps and moccasins and strings of beads. The squaws were gaudy in yellow-dyed smocks that they had produced from somewhere, high moccasins equipped with beaver tails and headbands studded with polished stones and bright shells.

A long column of warriors appeared ahead and came dashing up on decorated ponies, lances adorned with feathers and streamers. They obviously had come from the encampment whose smoke lay gray and prominent ahead. They were greeted by Gray Buffalo and his warriors and there was much ceremony and powwow.

"They're Cheyenne too," Mike told Nancy. "They came to act as a guard of honor to where they're taking us."

The presence of the two white prisoners aroused wild excitement among the visitors. They started to attempt the same intimidating tactics and acts of bravado that Mike had endured the previous day, but Gray Buffalo gave a command that put a stop to it.

"As I told you, Gray Buffalo swings a lot of weight," Mike commented to Nancy. "I've got a hunch that big outfit ahead is his real village. We're only a small section of it."

Esau Solomon aroused even greater comment and curiosity among the arrivals, but after discovering that he was attempting to qualify as a member of their tribe, they avoided him.

The arrivals flanked the column as the march was resumed westward. The distance was farther than Mike had estimated. It was sundown when they topped a long rise in the plain. Nancy uttered a small, despairing sound. The flat adjoining a stream was occupied by scores of Indian lodges. There was no telling their number, but there were more than two hundred, Mike estimated. A big herd of ponies grazed in the distance, under guard. The lodges of important chiefs faced a wide space near the center of the encampment. This was reserved for dancing, council fires and ceremonials.

Nancy looked at Mike with tragic eyes. "Now, we'll never get away," she choked. "There are too many of them. Hundreds."

Medicine men and ghost doctors came cavorting to meet their procession. Gray Buffalo led his small contingent into the big encampment. They circled the council square twice, then halted. Mike grunted in surprise.

"What is it?" Nancy asked.

"Ever hear of Sitting Bull? Or Crazy Horse? Or Two Moons?"

"Vaguely," she said. "Why?"

Mike indicated a line of important men, many in full regalia, who sat cross-legged reviewing the arriving procession. "That one with the square face and barrel-shaped body is Sitting Bull, top chief of the Uncpapa Sioux and probably the best brain in the Indian world. Crazy Horse is the one in only a breechclout and a single feather in his hair. He never goes in for fancy regalia. He's Sioux too, an Oglala. He is a fighter. Two Moons, the one in the steeple-crowned hat, is Cheyenne, one of their big chiefs."

"What does it mean?"

"This is a Cheyenne village. These lodges are Cheyenne, and they've been hereditary enemies of the Sioux for as long back as white men know. Now they're powwowing together, holding medicine talk."

Gray Buffalo dismounted, joined the waiting chiefs, and the pipe was passed with great and sober ceremony. That took a long time. Then Two Moons led all his guests into the biggest of the lodges.

Mike and Nancy moved along with Gray Buffalo's people to the fringe of the big camp where there was room for them to pitch their lodges. The squaws began the work, once more, of setting up the lodges. Nancy joined in the task.

On the surface, Mike seemed free to do what he pleased. In reality, every step he took was watched. Two new faces appeared as guards, replacing his previous sentries.

They were on foot, having turned their ponies over to young Cheyenne who led them away. The new guards stood within close reach, apparently ignoring Mike but obviously keenly alert with rifles ready in their arms.

Mike rubbed down the roan and the pack pony with wisps of grass and took his time at the task. That helped ease some of the tension that had been building up within him, even though it surprised the two animals. They were tough, plains horses with a lot of mustang in them and were not accustomed to such tender care. Mike's menial task at least amused the Cheyenne guards, who considered such activity as fit only for squaws.

Mike watched Nancy help Elk Woman and Snow Dove set the poles of the chief's lodge, unfurl the cover and lace it in place. Nancy seemed to enjoy the task. Mike comprehended that she preferred that activity to the strain of waiting — waiting for what? He knew their chances of ever leaving the village alive were very slim and he was sure she realized it also.

He was puzzled as to why he had been allowed to live thus far. He doubted that Esau was the answer, even though the black man believed he was their protestor. In the Indian scheme of things the big man was no more important at the moment than any of the young braves who were racing aimlessly around, getting into mischief, booting kick-balls, tormenting the squaws and acting generally like hoodlums. Esau had not yet passed the test. He was not yet a warrior.

There was little rest for anyone in the encampment that night. Dancing went on at many lodge fires. Drums and whistles kept sounding and there was a general air of excitement and anticipation that continued all through the hours of darkness.

It was not until well after the morning meal that the restlessness reached a climax. Suddenly, all the drums began booming at the council circle. A great dance was starting. The Indians formed a line and began shuffling in a huge circle around the central fire. Some dragged buffalo skulls. Others had long ropes attached to poles and laced around their chests. These were warriors clad only in breechclouts. All bore ugly scars on their chests and backs.

Nancy ignored Elk Woman's shrill demands for help at the lodge and joined Mike where he sat in the background. She settled down beside him, Indian-fashion on folded legs. He became suddenly angry. "Stop that!" he snapped. "You're not a squaw. Don't try to act like one!"

Anger flared in her and she was on the point of a blistering reply. Then, suddenly meek, she obeyed by shifting her position. "I'm sorry," she said. "I'll try to act like a civilized person — in your presence, at least."

The tempo of the drums became faster. Whistles sounded. A procession of Indians, fantastically painted, came dancing through the village, carrying a long pole. This they set in an opening in the center of the council circle. A small lodge, built rudely of brush, had been erected nearby.

A new contingent of Indians joined the dancers. "Sioux!" Mike murmured. "They're talking part in a Cheyenne initiation. That means they're allies."

"Is this part of the initiation you spoke about?"

"This is one way of becoming a first grade warrior. The toughest way. Those Indians dragging the buffalo skulls and poles didn't get those scars in battle. They got them in the Sun Dance. The real thing. Right now they're only pretending, only living over what they went through."

"How would they get such terrible wounds in a dance?"

"The Sun Dance isn't a pretty thing to see," Mike said. "It's a deeply religious rite.

It's usually danced at the beginning of summer, but it can be danced at other times if candidates ask for it when they want to become full-fledged warriors if a big fight is ahead."

"Then this means there's to be a fight?"

"That's my guess," Mike said.

She had a startling thought. "Snow Dove mentioned to me something about Esau being a candidate to go to the sun. I didn't understand at the time. Did she mean that . . . ?"

"I'm afraid so," Mike said. "That's why he's been without food, without water, without speaking to anyone. That's part of it."

"Where is he now?"

"Probably in that hut of brush, along with other Indians who will dance. That's the medicine lodge. The pole they set up is the medicine pole — the Sun Dance pole."

"Just what do they do?"

"Try to prove how long they can endure pain. These things last for hours — sometimes for days."

"And Esau is going to do that?"

"It seems that way."

She went silent, but remained beside him, watching as the shuffling dance continued. The drums never missed a throbbing note.

The squaws formed a second circle, and their voices joined in the chant.

Mike found himself responding, in spite of himself, to the hypnotic influence of the scene, to the color, the stomp of moccasins and the rhythm of the drums. The drumbeat seemed tuned to the throb of his pulse. He found himself wanting to get to his feet and join the chanting circle. The warriors and squaws moved now like images, their eyes fixed on the bare pole which seemed to have become the center of their universe.

He tore his gaze from the scene and found that Nancy had once again shifted to the squaw posture. In her eyes was the same fixed, faraway look that he knew had been in his own. He shook her roughly. The rapt expression faded. She gazed up at him, almost resentfully.

"Stop it!" he rasped. "Stop it! This stuff you're so fascinated with came from the Stone Age. The Dark Age. From hell itself."

The trancelike mood faded. She looked at him with that level inspection that he was learning to be a prelude to some unexpected change of subject. "Are you married?" she asked.

Mike was so taken aback, he could only glare at her. "Now, what's that got to do with this? And what girl in her right mind would marry a man like me? Colonel Cool calls me a renegade."

"You haven't answered my question, McVey."

Mike scowled at her. "What you really want to know is if I've been a squawman. That's it, isn't it?"

"You seem to know considerable about Indians," she said.

"I've traveled with Indian buffalo hunters, lived in their lodges when I was with the cavalry," Mike said. "That was when things were more peaceful. I picked up enough of the Cheyenne language and sign language to act as interpreter at parleys between the chiefs and the Army. Is that answer enough?"

"No."

"If I told you the truth, would you believe it?"

"Perhaps, although about all the men I've met are accomplished liars in regard to matters of the heart."

Mike grinned. "The answer is no. Oh, I've almost been corralled a couple of times. There's a very pretty gal in Cheyenne that I was taken with. In fact, I was on my way to Cheyenne last fall to find out if she was still fancy-free when — but that's another story. I was going to get hitched to a dazzler in Hays City, but she ran off with a shortcard sport. Then there was a high-stepper in Julesburg who —"

"Now, you are lying and trying to boast," she said. "I believe what you said at first. I also doubt if any girl would have you, Indian or white."

"Now it's my turn to ask a personal question," Mike said. "How long have you known Marsh Prine?"

"Marsh Prine? Why, from childhood. We grew up in the same town, were in the same school as children."

"You must think a great deal of him."

She eyed him speculatively. "Now, that really is getting personal, McVey."

"You're right," Mike said. "I apologize and withdraw the question. A woman would have to be considerably in love with a man to stand between him and a bullet like you did the night Esau tried to shoot him."

She seemed at loss for words for a time. She was staring at him, wide-eyed. "Did I say something wrong?" hc asked.

"Why — why, no," she said. "However, in addition to the question of how much I might have been in love with Marsh Prine, doesn't it occur to you that trying to prevent him from being killed was only a matter of common decency?"

"Now that's a matter-of-fact way of putting it," Mike said. "I just can't understand you."

"What can't you understand, Mr. McVey?"

"You can forget the mister part of it. My front handle is Mike. What I don't savvy is how you and a man like Prine — how you fell — oh, forget it."

"Exactly what are you trying to say, Mike McVey?"

She was leaning very near to make herself heard above the chanting, the stomping and the eagle whistles. She was too near, too attractive. He could not resist the temptation. He kissed her on the lips. They were soft, yielding. He even fancied that they clung for a moment.

He drew abruptly away. "Damn Marsh Prine!" he exploded.

"Don't blame Marsh Prine!" she said. "It was all your idea. You shouldn't have done that. It's in bad taste to do such things in public in Indian villages. Look, the squaws are pointing fingers at us, shaming us."

"To hell with the squaws!" Mike snarled. "If it's a gentleman you want, you've got him. I'd never qualify."

"That's for certain. Michael McVey, a gentleman? Perish the thought. I admit you've put on a little polish since the first time I saw you when you were being thrown

160

from a horse into the mud, but I can't imagine you decked out in spats, a top hat and cutaway with a gates-ajar collar."

Mike had to grin. "You said the right thing. Perish the thought."

"You're not nearly as homely as I first believed, now that you shave occasionally. You looked like a thin and hungry bear that day. You're also much younger than I believed. You're not a great deal older than I, are you?"

"How old are you?"

"There's another point against you. No real gentleman would ask a lady that question. I'm past twenty-three."

"You *are* getting along in years," Mike said. "I'm four or five years older than you, which gives me the advantage of age. Well, the squaws have stopped pointing at us. The feature event is about to start. You better go into Gray Buffalo's lodge and don't look out."

"I'll wait," she said. "If the squaws can stand the sight of whatever is going to happen, I believe I can too."

A dozen chiefs and subchiefs, in full regalia, appeared from the lodges and seated themselves at the council circle. The chanting abruptly took on a new quality. The beat of the drums did not seem to change, the monotonous chant of the "e ya, e ya, e ya," went on. But both *had* changed. There was a deeper, grimmer tone to the sounds, a lustful, thirsty note. An anticipation.

Four withered oldsters in horns and grotesque masks and painted bodies came prancing into the circle, the chanters opening paths for them. These medicine men stomped and cavorted around the pole.

They finally danced to the entrance of the medicine lodge. They finished their display with a final united screech that was followed by silence in the village. Dead silence. The dancers stood motionless.

Men began to appear from the medicine lodge. There were eight of them. One was Esau Solomon. Like the others, he wore only a breechclout. Like the others, he had a great, yellow semblance of the sun painted on his chest and on his back. All their faces and bodies were stained a death-pallor gray, with skeletonlike teeth painted around their mouths.

They stood in a file. Warriors now moved in, one for each applicant. They had sharpened knives in their hands. Mike watched Esau. The Cheyenne who was to be his sponsor stood before him, making obeisance to the gods of the four winds. Then the warrior grasped a fold of flesh on Esau's

162

chest, thrust the knife through until it emerged. Blood flowed.

Nancy uttered a little moaning outcry. She was pale and horrified, but she seemed unable to avert her eyes.

Esau's sponsor had in his belt a wooden skewer which he thrust through the perforation he had made in the flesh. To its ends he quickly tied long thongs of rough, plaited buffalo leather. The opposite ends of the thongs were looped to the medicine pole.

Skewers were placed in the bodies of the seven other applicants at the same time by their sponsors. Three of them had elected to have the instruments of ordeal thrust through the flesh of their backs. To these skewers were attached thongs which had rock-weighted buffalo skulls dragging at the ends. Like Esau, the other four were united with the medicine pole.

The sponsors stepped back, their initial grim task completed. During their task no sound came from the onlookers, and, above all, from the candidates. To have uttered any sign of suffering or weakness would have disgraced the applicant.

The silence ended. Some signal had been given. Every Indian voice in the village broke into a moaning chant. But they stood motionless.

The applicants began to dance around the pole. They sat their heels hard into the ground, leaning back against the ropes that held the skewers wedged in their bodies and began circling the pole. The three with the buffalo skulls dragging, moved with them. All kept staring at the sun, eyes wide.

"How long?" Nancy asked hollowly.

"Until they tear the sticks from their flesh," Mike said.

"You said that might take hours — even days."

"Yes."

"What if they never tear free?"

Mike did not answer that. "You — you mean they would die there?" she asked.

"That happens too."

"It's monstrous! Inhuman! If you were any kind of a man you would cut Esau Solomon free."

"If I did that he'd be completely disgraced, looked on as a weakling, worse than a squaw. He doesn't dare utter a word of pain, or any sign of complaint."

She arose and ran wildly to Gray Buffalo's lodge, disappearing into its shelter. Mike drew his palms along the sides of his breeches, rubbing away the ice-cold sweat. But the moisture kept reappearing. He wanted to run too, run and hide from this sight. But he did not. He owed that to Esau, who had once saved his life and had nearly lost his own in doing so.

That had happened when Mike was in the cavalry and Esau had been a swamper for a civilian freighter who had contracted to haul supplies by bulltrain to Army posts on the Bozeman Trail. Mike, with a cavalry detachment, was escorting the bulltrain when it was ambushed by a superior force of Shoshones. There was a scar on Esau's back that would last a lifetime — as long as any scars he might sustain from the Sun Dance. That was where he had taken the blow of a war hatchet that a Shoshone warrior had swung to brain Mike as he lay helpless beneath his fallen horse. An arrow had pinned Esau's right arm to his side, and his left arm had been broken by a blow from a club. He had staggered in, taking the blow from the hatchet in his back, saving Mike's life.

"We are frien's," Esau had explained days later when he finally turned the corner in the Army hospital at Fort Phil Kearny and was firmly on his way to recovery. "He treated me like a man should be treated. He'd have done the same fer me."

Mike, that coldness on his palms, and in his stomach, sat watching Esau circle the medicine pole, leaning with all his weight

165

against the torture bonds. Blood ran down his body. It stained his moccasins. He leaned heavier, staring at the sun. The skewers refused to burst through his flesh and free him from this torment. Like his great heart, his fibers were too powerful, too unyielding.

The chant went on. Mike was again caught up in its spell. It was now the Sun Dance song, at first seeming to be no different than the other chants. Yet it was different.

E ya ha we ye he he
Ye ye he ye ho we ye

On and on and on. The sun passed the zenith. It had been mid-morning when all this had started. Two warriors burst free, then another. Their ordeal was over. One of the remaining applicants began to reel drunkenly, dazed and about to fall. His sponsor moved in, seized him by the shoulders and added his own full strength to that of the candidate. That freed the Cheyenne. Freed him forever. He was torn away from the skewer. Before the blood could be staunched he died there, died a warrior who would be acclaimed in song and legend, for he died without a sign of weakness or of knowing pain.

166

The four remaining candidates reeled by the body, unheeding. One, who was dragging buffalo skulls, broke free, and friends and relatives helped him away to treat his injuries. He would recover to wear the feather of a warrior. Another, bound by the thongs to the medicine pole, also succeeded and was saved.

Only Esau and a Cheyenne were left. Finally, the Cheyenne could no longer endure the torture and gave up. He freed himself from the thongs and the skewer and slunk away, shunned by his disgraced family and friends. He mounted a pony and rode off into the plains. He would never show his face again to those who had known him.

The chant went on. Esau danced the terrible rigadoon alone. A single drum now sounded the beat, keeping time to the slowing push of Esau's heart. Mercifully, an overcast had moved in, and the westering sun was only a dim, pale disk. Otherwise the big man might have been blinded. He was spared that, at least. But not the pain. His face was a contorted study in agony. He was a man in hell, sinking deeper into the pit of torment.

Mike heard a hysterical voice screaming. Nancy raced past him, a knife in her hand. He aroused from the drugged apathy into which he had fallen and ran to halt her — too late. Still screaming unintelligible words that Mike believed were those of the Lord's Prayer, she slashed the thongs that held Esau to the pole of torture.

He fell soggily. Nancy let the knife drop to the bloodstained soil. She stood, tears of pity streaming down her cheeks, looking down at the unconscious black man.

Warriors seized her, screeching furious threats. They would have slain her on the spot, but Mike rushed in, shouting in Cheyenne. She had committed the ultimate sacrilege, and he knew that someone would have to pay the penalty. A mere squaw, and a white one at that, had desecrated the sacred Sun Dance rite by interfering.

A frenzied warrior swung a club, intending to brain the girl. Mike parried the blow and hurled the warrior back. Others crowded in, brandishing knives and clubs. He spoke frantically in the smattering of Cheyenne he had learned.

"The code!" he shouted. "The warrior's code! It was not Man-of-the-Night's fault the girl interfered. She does not understand your ways. No warrior should be weak enough to kill a woman who did not know what she was doing. Man-of-the-Night must be allowed to continue pleasing the gods of the medicine pole. If he cannot do so, then some friend of his must take his place. That is the way. That is the law."

The tumult faded. Gray Buffalo pushed to the front. In the background, the guest chiefs had got to their feet and were watching in silence. This was a Cheyenne affair. They waited to see how their hosts handled such a traditional matter.

Esau lay where he had fallen. Mike knelt beside him. "Man-of-the-Night!" Then he spoke again. "Esau!"

Esau did not respond. Nancy knelt also. She was sobbing. She tore the sleeves from her tattered gown and used the cloth to bandage and stem the blood from the big man's wounds.

Mike saw that Esau would never be able to finish the Sun Dance. At least finish it and live. He got to his feet. He knew the code. He had proclaimed it himself. The ordeal could be finished to the bitter end, either by Esau or a brother. If there was no brother, then a friend could come forward. Otherwise Esau would be banished in disgrace, perhaps even stoned to death to appease the gods. Interference by a woman in the ceremonial must be atoned.

Mike stripped off his hide shirt. He picked up the skewer that had been drawn from Esau's flesh and made the sign that he would continue the dance in his friend's place. For a space there was complete silence as the Indians stared. Then the sponsor who had performed the duty on Esau stepped forward with his knife in his hand.

He seized a ridge of flesh on Mike's chest. Mike braced himself, gazing toward the dim sun. He felt the hot, stabbing pain of the knife, felt the sickening agony as the skewer was inserted.

Nancy, busy caring for the unconscious big man, now became aware of what was going on. She came to her feet. "No!" she choked. "Oh, no, no, no! Dear God, no!"

Squaws seized her and she was lost among a shouting throng of Indians. Mike stood as thongs were looped to the medicine pole and attached to the skewer. Then the drum resumed its beat. He could still hear Nancy screaming hysterically somewhere in the village. He began the dance — the traditional shuffling step around the medicine pole, leaning against the skewer.

All the warriors began the Sun Dance chant, their voices low, muffled. Except for that and the throb of the drum, and Nancy's distant screaming, the whole world seemed to have gone silent — waiting. Every ear was listening for some sound of protest, of suffering, or of weakness from the white man.

Mike kept his gaze fixed on the wan sun. That was the traditional posture. The sun was still more than an hour's time above the horizon, and he knew that even after it had set there would be no surcease for him. The ordeal must go on until victory, surrender — or death — came.

The pain was a fire inside him. He had the bitter disadvantage of not believing in this primitive rite. He did not believe in their gods, or that he would be rewarded by them for his ordeal. Religious fervor had added ten-fold strength to the other candidates, deadened their senses. But all of his body was tortured.

He knew he could not last much beyond sundown. He would die. He must break free. He *must!* He moved a stride toward the medicine pole, loosening the thongs, then hurled himself back with all his weight.

He failed. He was unable to tear the skewers free. The scene swam before his eyes. He fought for consciousness. To have fainted would have been the ultimate disaster, both for Esau and himself.

He managed to keep moving, shuffling his feet mechanically until his head cleared. He saw the circle of faces. Gray Buffalo was there, watching. And Sitting Bull. And Crazy Horse. Two Moons, the great chief of the Northern Cheyenne. Gall of the Uncpapa Sioux. They had seen many Sun Dances, but they had never seen one like this. They had never seen a white man dance. They stood watching with inscrutable eyes.

Mike saw another face in the background. Nancy. She was standing among squaws who were seeing to it that she did not again interfere with the sacred dance. She had her eyes fixed on him. They were dark and brooding against the dead pallor of her skin. Her lips were moving. He knew she was praying for him.

That did something for him. Inspired him. He steeled himself for another effort to free himself from this circle of agony. A supreme effort. He moved to the medicine pole, used it as a base to give himself more power, and hurled himself to the full length of the thongs. This time, he tore free. A blast of pain exploded through him, but he was also aware of a sense of high accomplishment and rejoicing — and of gratitude and humbleness.

He fell to the ground beside Esau who still lay there, too weak to rise. Nancy broke free of restraining hands and came rushing to them. Sobbing, she began caring for Mike's torn flesh. Snow Dove arrived and knelt beside Esau.

"Why?" Nancy kept moaning. "Why did you do it?"

Neither Mike nor Esau answered. Even if they had been able to speak, there was no answer for that question, at least one that could be put into words.

Chapter 8

Mike and Esau sat in a lodge huddling close to a warming fire. Wind vibrated the walls of the shelter, and the poles creaked. It was a shabby, small lodge, the covering a patchwork of old buffalo leather and remnants of army tents. The poles were crooked cripples that had been salvaged from discards of better lodges. It had been assembled by Nancy and Snow Dove. It was now the home of Nancy and Mike and Esau.

On the face of it, the Cheyenne had given them a free hand since the events of the Sun Dance. In reality they were more closely guarded than before. They had been ordered to maintain their own lodge because by keeping them together it was easier to watch them. Even though Esau ostensibly held the status of a warrior, it was evident he was still on probation. They did not trust him. At least two experienced warriors were always close at hand to watch every step any of them took outside their hovel.

Ten days or more had passed since the Sun Dance. Their injuries were healing.

Mike was emerging from the apathy that had held him weak and listless for days because of loss of blood. Esau also had been stricken with the same cause. Nancy and Snow Dove had fed and cared for them during those days when they had lingered between life and death. They had seen to it that both of them had lived through it.

Mike caught occasional glimpses of Nancy as the wind whipped the door curtain. She was working with the Cheyenne women outside, flensing buffalo hides. A hunt had been successful, and the squaws were busy jerking meat and preparing the hides. Once more the sky was gray, the wind cold. Winter was reluctant to surrender the plains. Heavy rains had again drenched the land.

Nancy, using a scraper made of an animal's jawbone, worked steadily, flensing the inner side of a buffalo hide, clearing it of all flesh, and thinning it so that it would be more easily softened by the mixture of tannic and dye that would be used by older Cheyenne women to convert it into robes. Other hides were being shorn of hair as well in order to form leather for clothing or lodge coverings.

Snow Dove and Elk Woman worked with Nancy. She wore a fringed smock over a cotton blouse and a petticoat. Her hair was held with a beaded elkskin band. Her skin had tanned. Except for her coppery hair she could have been taken for a Cheyenne.

She and Snow Dove talked animatedly as they worked. Nancy was picking up the language rapidly, and she and the Cheyenne girl seemed to find much to gossip about. Elk Woman occasionally joined in the conversation.

"What's in their mind?" Mike asked Esau, breaking a long silence. "The Cheyenne? What are they up to?"

"We goin' to know before long," Esau said. "We movin' out as soon as dey are finished wid de meat an' hidin'."

"How do you know?"

"Snow Dove tell me. We goin' wid Gray Buffalo's village, same as we did 'afore we joned dis big one."

"Now why would Gray Buffalo start wandering around again with just a few lodges?"

"I don' know, but I reckon we'll find out. Dar's one thing fer sure. You an' me an' Miss Nancy are goin' to be right in de middle of whatever dey're up to."

"I've been wondering why Roscoe Cool hasn't done something about trying to get her back?"

"De colonel has give her up as daid."

"Now how do you know that?"

"De Cheyenne know. Dar's reservation Injuns acrost de river dat keep de chiefs on this side info'med as to what goes on at de fo't. Snow Dove tells me things. De squaws know everythin'. De colonel's got strict orders from Gineral Sheridan not to take any risks. De colonel waited, hopin' to hear from you. When he didn't, he figured you was dead too by dis time. So he's just done nothin'. Dat's what he's best at — doin' nothin'. But it seemed to upset whatever de Cheyenne had planned. Dat time Gray Buffalo wandered around fer days without settlin' down befo' we come here to camp wid dis big village, wasn't jest fer exercise. Injuns don' like extra wor' unless it's worth while."

"Am I thinking along the same line you are?" Mike asked. "Is that why Sitting Bull and Crazy Horse and Gall were in camp that night before the Sun Dance?"

"Maybe so. An' I got a hunch de Cheyenne has got some plans fer you."

"For me?"

"Dar's somethin' mighty big, an' mighty ugly in de wind, an' I figger it ain't goin' to do dem soldiers at de fo't any good if it works. Snow Dove says dar's more Injuns hangin' around dis country dan she's got hairs in her haid. She tol' me dar was more visitin' chiefs in de village to smoke de pipe, while we was under de weather. Nez Percé, Shoshone, even de Ute, Scarcheek. Ute country is a long way off, but dar's a Ute war party near, Snow Dove says."

"The tribes aren't mobbing up around here, just to watch the Sun Dance or hunt buffalo," Mike said. "But Roscoe Cool ought to know all about it. After all, he's got competent scouts to keep an eye on things. And there are always Indians who sell information for a dollar or two in whisky or trade."

"Dar's always a bait to ketch the smartest fish," Esau said. "All you got to do is find de right kind o' bait. De colonel might have give up the missy an' you as daid, but he's still anxious to make a name fer hisself, 'specially now dat de Army's goin' to send Gineral Custer in wid de 7th Cavalry."

"Are they really going to do that?"

"Seems like it's official. When Gineral Custer comes in, Colonel Cool will be only small potatoes 'less he does somethin' to make a big man o' hisself mighty quick. De Injun chiefs know dis. Dey know all about such things. Dey got jealousy an' ambition in dar own villages."

"You forgot to mention one item," Mike

said. "Cool might have given up Nancy Halstead as dead, but there's another person on this side of the river he'd like to get his hands on. It'd be a big feather in his cap. You know who I mean."

"I know," Esau said.

"Then you also know what would happen to you if they caught you. They'd make you pay in ways you can't imagine."

He turned. Nancy had entered the lodge, unheard, and had been listening. "You must go away, Esau," she said. "Far away, where they would never find you."

"Whar would dat be?" Esau asked.

"Canada, if need be. That's not far away. Or maybe you'd prefer Mexico."

"Dis country is my home," Esau said. "I stay here."

Mike was eying Nancy with mock surprise. "This is an odd way for the victim of this outrage to talk. You're trying to help your kidnaper get away."

"The whole thing was a terrible mistake," she said. "Esau must get away while he has the chance. Staying here is foolish."

"My name, missy," Esau said, "is Man-of-the-Night."

Nancy sighed and made a helpless gesture. On that point there was no meeting of their minds. Esau was still Cheyenne, proud of his status as a warrior, even though he had not yet been unconditionally accepted.

"It doesn't matter what name you want to go by," Nancy argued. "Mike just told you what would happen if they caught you."

"Dey won't ketch me," Esau said. He added, "Alive."

That silenced her. After a moment Mike broke that silence. "You wouldn't fight them, Esau," he said. "You know that. After all, a lot of the troopers at the fort are your friends. Some of them were in that fight on Warbonnet when you saved my bacon. They saw you do it. But they'd have to carry out orders. You can't fight men you campaigned with."

Esau did not answer for a long time. "I a Cheyenne now," he said stolidly. "Dey my people."

There was no more talk for a long time in the shabby little lodge. Nancy braised buffalo meat on spits over the fire.

"We move tomorrow," she said.

Mike paused in the act of eating. "So soon? But they're not finished making meat. Where are we going?"

"I don't know, but Snow Dove was crying on my shoulder a while ago when none of the other squaws were around."

"Crying? Indian girls don't cry."

"That's not so. They have feelings the same as everyone else. The same emotions. Because of the hard life they live they learn not to show them, but they have them bottled up inside. Even Elk Woman is sad. I'm sure she'd like to cry on somebody's shoulder too. She really isn't as tough and heartless as she tries to be. She's worried about Gray Buffalo. She has great affection for him, and he for her. They've been married a long time. He's never taken a second wife. And the other Cheyenne women are upset also."

"What's your opinion, Esau?" Mike asked.

"Big fight comin'," Esau said. "Squaws think lots o' Cheyenne goin' to de Great Spirit."

"You think Cool will — ?"

Esau made a gesture for caution. He motioned toward the walls. "Dem two dar outside are listenin'," he murmured. "Dey understand English."

Mike saw shadows against the thin walls. The two Indians who had been assigned to stand watch over them had moved in close, and were eavesdropping.

Nancy spoke softly. "Snow Dove's tears are for you, Esau."

"What you say, missy?" Esau mumbled, startled.

"You heard me. She's afraid — for you. You're a warrior in the tribe now, you know. If there's a battle, you'll be in it."

"I loved Ruth," Esau said shakily.

"Of course. Snow Dove loved her too. They were sisters. She would make you a good wife. You would not be lonely any longer. It's not good for a man like you to be alone — or to live for vengeance."

"I ain't listenin' to talk like dat," Esau said. "I made a promise I'd make him pay fer Ruth."

"You've got to quit living for vengeance alone," Nancy said. "Ruth is gone to the Great Spirit. Nothing can change that. You'll only destroy your own soul by living only to kill Marshall Prine."

Esau's face had softened a little at the revelation of Snow Dove's affection. But it hardened again at the mention of Prine's name. He arose abruptly, wrapped a blanket around his shoulders and left the lodge, striding away into the early darkness.

"It's over," Mike said after a long silence.

"What's over?" she asked.

"Esau's vendetta against your doctor. Esau likely won't admit it, but you've won."

"How do you know that?"

"I just know it. I know Esau. He would never harm Marsh Prine now. You can rest easy on that score, at least. I wonder if Marsh will ever really know how much you've done for him?"

She eyed him, and seemed about to bring up a subject he believed had been in her mind for a long time. He had no idea what it was. And once again she decided to let it pass. "If I've saved Marsh Prine from anything, I've also saved Esau Solomon, if what you say is true and that it's all over as far as the vendetta is concerned," she said. "I'm speaking of Esau's soul. He'll never be a Cheyenne at heart, no matter what. He would never forgive himself now if he carried out his vengeance and killed Marsh. It would haunt him the rest of his life. I only hope and pray that you're right and that I have really won out."

Two Cheyenne warriors suddenly burst into the lodge. They seized Nancy and marched her out of the shabby quarters. From the entrance, Mike watched her being taken to Gray Buffalo's big lodge, evidently to be quartered there under the eyes of the chief and Elk Woman.

When Esau returned he was also barred and told to put up at the lodge of the surly couple with whom he and Mike had been housed originally. That left Mike alone.

But not for long. The two Cheyenne

guards entered, spread robes on the floor and settled down for the night. They soon fell asleep, or pretended to sleep. Mike was unguarded. He debated it a long time, knowing that he was being offered a chance to escape. Why? Finally he turned in and slept. There were reasons why he had decided not to accept the offer — at the moment at least.

They were on the march again by mid-morning. Camp had been broken without haste, but the pall of sadness and tension that Nancy had brought up, was palpably growing heavier. There was little chatter among the Cheyenne women, and no laughter at all.

Esau rode with the warriors, but Mike's two horses had been appropriated, and he and Nancy were forced to walk now whether he wanted to or not. He was prodded along at times by the lance points of the two Cheyenne who evidently were no longer only guarding him, but, Mike surmised, had been told to make life as miserable for him as possible.

The day was raw and overcast with the promise of more rain. The procession moved in a northeasterly direction across a plain of hummocky bunch and buffalo grass.

"I'm sure the Missouri River isn't far ahead," Mike told Nancy on one of the few occasions when he could speak to her out of hearing of the two Cheyenne.

Snow Dove walked with Nancy the greater part of the time. There were no more tears, but, like the other Cheyenne women, she was sober and depressed. Not so the men. Their mood was just the opposite. They were inwardly boiling with excitement and expectation. Now and then one would utter a warwhoop, brandish a knife or lance and strike down an imaginary foe.

"They expect a fight, sure enough," Mike told Nancy. "Do you suppose Roscoe Cool has crossed the river with the troops?"

That theory exploded late that afternoon when they crested a rise that afforded a long view ahead. Several miles away stretched the thin brush line of the big river — the Missouri.

"I know where we are now," Mike told Nancy when a halt was called. "Once you're across, it's only half a day's ride to Fort Flagg. By river it's considerably farther, of course. Esau's farm is down the river quite a ways."

"You've been in this country enough to know it that well?"

"I came this way a couple of weeks ago with the gold and —"

"The gold?"

Mike rapped his forehead with his knuckles. It had been a bad slip of the tongue, but the words could not be recalled now.

"That was just a little joke of mine," he said lamely.

"Joke? I'd say you look like a red-faced, thick-skulled person who had just let a big, fat cat out of the bag. You have found gold somewhere, haven't you? How much?"

"Not much."

"Exactly how much?"

"How would I know? I didn't have a scales with me. All I could do was balance it on a pole across a log with me on the other end."

"Good gracious! Quit keeping me in suspense! How much did it weigh?"

"Around three hundred pounds as best I could figure it."

"Three hundred *pounds?* Of gold? Why, that's a fortune!"

"Not quite," Mike said. "But it would make a nice stake."

"Where is it?"

"Ask me no more questions," Mike said. "I might not tell the truth."

"You'd make a very poor liar, McVey, even

if you tried. You've got what might be called an open, readable map for a face. I might even go so far as to say you have an honest face. Too bad you haven't got a mind to match."

"Are you trying to say that I haven't been honest with you?"

"Exactly. When are you going to make your getaway from this village?"

"I *must* be easy to read," Mike complained. "How did you know?"

"It hasn't been entirely guesswork. It's sort of been written all over you. But you keep delaying. Why? When are you going to make the break?"

"The word is 'we', not 'you,'" Mike said. "When I go we both go."

"I was afraid that was it," she said. "It can't be that way, Mike. They're watching me more closely than ever. If you get the chance, take it."

"I've had plenty of chances. I'm convinced they want me to walk away. One reason I haven't taken advantage of it is that I've wanted to make sure what they have in mind. It's part of the reason why they've let me live. Esau might have had something to do with keeping them from killing me at first, but they've had something else in mind for days."

"Such as?"

"I'm convinced they're setting a trap for Cool, and this village is the bait. Gray Buffalo has been parading this small party around for some time now, with Esau and you as the chief exhibits. The colonel has civilian scouts. They own field glasses. They must have spotted this party. If so, they surely know Esau is with it. He's too big to be mistaken. They may have identified you also, but there's a bigger chance they haven't — or at least aren't sure. You're dressed like the squaws."

"But the colonel hasn't taken the bait?"

"That seems to be the trouble. There's always the chance that even Esau hasn't been spotted and that they figure this is an unimportant hunting party not worth bothering with. The Cheyenne have friends over there among reservation Indians who hang around the fort. Snow Dove told Esau that Cool is convinced both you and I are dead. That's where I think I come in."

"In what way?"

"I'm not being guarded in any sense of the word. Not for the past two or three days. The two stonefaces who used to dog every step I made now wander out of sight and pretend to sleep as sound as logs in my lodge at night. Sometimes I think they really are asleep. I've been given every opportunity to slip away."

"But I don't see why —"

"The tribes can't waste much more time waiting for Cool to take the bait. They've got to start hunting buffalo in earnest before long and the real herds are far west of here as a rule. They've got to prod the colonel into putting his foot into the trap. I believe I'm to be allowed to escape so I can carry the word to the fort that you are alive, and a prisoner in this small village and that Esau is here, too. It would be too big a temptation. Cool would hardly pass it up."

"But wouldn't the Cheyenne know that you would also warn him it was a trap?"

"After all, as far as they're concerned, we do not know it's a trap. And maybe it isn't. Except for that one big village where the Sun Dance was held, we haven't really seen any mobilization of Indians. It's all circumstantial evidence. They also know Cool. They figure that he couldn't resist the bait, even if he was warned. He's got stars in his eyes. A general's stars. That often blinds a man's judgment, makes him deaf to advice. They are sure he'd very much like to make a name for himself before George Armstrong Custer is sent in."

"You've got to pull out," she said. "To-night. You've got to warn Cool. It *is* a trap. I know it. The Cheyenne have been expecting a fight for several days. A big fight."

"I can't leave you here," Mike said.

"You'll have to. You can't let hundreds of men be massacred. That would be monstrous."

Again the Cheyenne separated them, marching Nancy roughly away, prodding Mike in the opposite direction. The travois creaked into motion again, the ponies prodded by switches in the hands of the squaws. They moved toward the river. Rain struck them coldly in the face. They bent against it. As dreary twilight came the lodges were pitched on a flat not far from the great river.

The Missouri was high and swift and evidently still rising fast. Mike peered at the broad expanse that swept by. The water was the color of dirty bronze. The river was too high to be forded by laden cavalry horses and troopers. Mike decided that might be the reason why Cool had not yet taken the bait. Nature had interceded to delay him, perhaps. But he could still cross. He had steamboats at his disposal.

Chapter 9

Mike sat in the shabby little lodge after dark, faced with the great, heartrending decision of his life. He was alone. His Cheyenne guards had brought food from the cookfires of other lodges. They had shared with him in the crowded shelter, but now had wandered out into the village and had not returned. Once more the path to escape was being blatantly offered. It was typical of the Indian mind, which could be bewilderingly obtuse and complex in thinking and planning on one hand, and then childishly transparent and direct on the other.

He kept desperately searching his mind for some way out that would at least give him surcease from the torment of mind and soul that tore at him. It always came back to the harsh fact. He had no choice. He had to warn Roscoe Cool. If he left here tonight alone, he felt that he would never see Nancy alive again. She knew that also. He had seen it in her face that afternoon when the Cheyenne guards had interrupted their last talk and had hurried her away.

It had to be tonight. He could delay no longer. The patience of the Cheyenne would have an end. They would realize there was a reason why he kept rejecting such an obvious path to freedom. A bullet or a war ax in the brain would be his reward.

"I'll come back!" He spoke it fervently aloud. Nancy could not hear it. Not with her ears, but he believed implicitly that she was hearing it in her heart. She knew he was in love with her, a love he could not speak because she had been promised to Marshall Prine.

He had to do this thing. He must go away and leave her to face the whims of primitive passions and savage beliefs. It was one life against the lives of scores or hundreds of men. The one life that really meant everything to him, the center of his world.

He spoke hoarsely, "God forgive me. And God help me!"

He ripped a slit in the rear wall of the patchwork lodge. Wrapping a blanket around him, he crept out into the night. No voice raised an alarm. No dog had been brought with this village to raise a challenge.

He looked toward Gray Buffalo's lodge. Shadows moved against the lighted inner surface. He fancied that one of those shadows was Nancy's. Then he moved on through the rain, and that was the only memory of her he could carry with him.

He traveled fast. He still had not regained his full strength since the ordeal of the Sun Dance, but desperation filled in the gap. The raw scars on his chest throbbed with the effort. He moved at an elbow-swinging half-run until his lungs protested, then dropped into a walk until he had revived. Then he would repeat the process.

There was no sign of pursuit. He felt sure there would be none. He left the river which started a swing east that would have added miles to the distance, as he remembered the area. He was gambling against the possibility of losing direction entirely. There was nothing by which to judge his position, no stars, no sky. Only the ever-present chill rain. The storm had come in from the north, he remembered. So he kept the wind and the driving rain at his back, trusting that it had not shifted.

In the blackness he fell at times, sprawling over grass hummocks or clumps of brush or rocks. That was part of the hazards of the pace he was setting. He had no time to be careful.

His one great fear was that he might fall over the lip of a ravine or a cutbank to injury or even death. He tried to decipher the shadows ahead of him. On two occasions he was warned in time and managed to slide down precipitous banks and land on his feet with no broken bones. These gulches were carrying water in their pockets. In one gully, he was forced to swim fast for a dozen strokes across a current that threatened to carry him into trouble in the darkness. He managed to escape from the drag of the swift water and claw his way to the doubtful safety of the flat above. There he lay for minutes, spent, before being able to get to his feet and push ahead.

Always he had in mind the greater test he must face. Somewhere ahead, if he was on the right course, he would encounter the Missouri again. It must be crossed by a desperate man who had left everything he valued in life behind him, by a man who was spending what strength he had in a race through blackness in the hope he might get back to her side in time to perhaps save her. Save her for what? For Marshall Prine?

He had lost all cohesion with time and distance when he returned to it again — the river. The savage Missouri. He came upon it abruptly. Even in the starless darkness there was a luminescence about it. It lay athwart his path, dark and powerful, beckoning him. It whispered and sighed. It sounded a siren song. It dared him to test its strength. It stretched blackly into the night. His eyes could not make out the far shore.

He had no way of knowing what lay downstream. The rain, drumming on the river, wiped out all other sounds. There might be rapids not far below, or snags and rocks that would batter an exhausted man and let him drift down into the depths to his death.

He had to take the chance. Here was as good a place as any to continue the gamble which had begun the night he had told Roscoe Cool he would do his best to find Marsh Prine's promised bride and bring her back safely.

He stripped and tied his clothing and moccasins on his back and waded into the cold Missouri. He had been a strong swimmer from boyhood. He did not make the mistake of striking out at full strength, saving that for a possible moment when great effort might be needed. He stroked underhand, a slow method, but economical of wind and muscle. He was in an eddy that carried him swiftly away from shore. Looking back, he found that the point from which he had started was only a vague shadow and seemed far away.

He struck out overhand and won clear of the eddy which would have swung him back toward his starting point. He found himself in heavy current. At least that gave him a guide, and he swam crosswise of it. He was carried into churning cross rips where foam was thrown high as conflicting currents clapped ghostly hands.

He was tumbled down a short rapids, and struck an obstruction with an impact that jarred him. He let himself be carried limply along into quieter water. He let down his feet and found bottom. He now made out the loom of the east shore.

He staggered over slippery rocks, falling often, rising and floundering ahead until he emerged from the grasp of the river. He lay on the muddy bank until he could arise. The great Missouri swept by in the darkness, still savage in its might, but he had beaten it — this time.

He donned his clothing. It was soaked, but it at least tempered in a small measure the chill bite of the wind. He ran, flailing his arms. Circulation began to warm him a trifle.

He had no way of knowing the distance, but he kept placing one foot ahead of the other, for he had to get to Fort Flagg — and it was somewhere along the river.

He finally came abruptly into a clearing, and saw the ruins of a pole corral. The majority of the posts had been yanked down. He made out the debris of a burned cabin and smokehouse. The rain had revived the dank odor of charred wood.

He laughed wildly, although it sounded more like sobbing. This had been Esau's place, where he had intended to spend his life, growing his crops, raising a family and living in the glow of a loving wife.

This was where it had all started. Nearby was the gully where he had cached the gold. A small stream was running in the gully's bottom, but the gold was well above that threat. At any rate, there was no time for looking after cached gold, nor for mourning Esau's lost hopes. He knew now the distance to Fort Flagg. That gave him new strength.

He began running. He kept it up until the few lights of the settlement and the fort appeared ahead. The night was gone. Wan day was being born on the horizon. The rain had ended, but every frond of grass and finger of brush lashed his legs with cold wetness. The civilian settlement was drab and sleeping. The turrets and stockade of the fort stood like the battlements of a castle against the dismal sky.

Except for barges and a collection of small craft, the steamboat landing was empty.

Both the *Far Frontier* and the *Far West* were gone. The stockade gate of the fort was closed. A sentry challenged him from the parapet as he came running out of the darkness.

"Halt, or I'll shoot!"

Mike was too spent to make himself understood for a time. The sentry called for help, and Mike heard the sergeant-of-the-guard come running from the orderly room.

"It's a blasted Injun, from the looks, sarge," the sentry said. "But he seems to be tryin' to speak English. Should I put a slug in him?"

The sergeant was Pete Jenkins. "My God, it's Lieutenant McVey!" he exclaimed. "Hold your fire, you ninny. He's no Indian, even if he's dressed like one."

The small gate in the stockade was opened, and Mike entered. He was now able to speak coherently. The post was dark and sleeping. This was as it should be, but it seemed to him that it was too silent, too devoid of activity. Little sound came from the stables beyond the parade ground where the horses should now be stirring, eager for their morning ration of hay and grain.

"I want to speak to the colonel, Jenkins," he said.

"At this hour?"

"Yes, yes! Hurry, man! Take me to his quarters! It's important. I've got to start back as quick as possible! I've got to get back to —"

He realized the futility of telling these men that he had to go back to Gray Buffalo's village and return to captivity, that he had to get back to Nancy's side, that he had to be with her no matter what happened. They would never understand.

"Anyway, Colonel Cool ain't here," the sergeant said. "He's out in the field with the boys."

"In the field? Where?"

"That ain't for me to say," Jenkins protested.

"Who's in charge here?" Mike demanded desperately.

"Why — why, I reckon it's Dr. Prine. A couple o' young doctors came in to git frontier experience an' they went with the regiment while Dr. Prine stayed at the fort to look after them that's in the infirmary."

"Prine? In command? He's no line officer."

"No, sir, but Lieutenant Biggs, what was left as senior officer, come down with the ague an' is bedded in the infirmary. It gits him in wet weather. Dr. Prine holds captain's rank as a surgeon, an', bein' no other commissioned officer is here I reckon he's in charge."

A sudden horrifying thought hit Mike. "My God, Pete, Cool isn't moving against the Cheyenne, is he? Don't tell me he's taken the regiment across the river? The steamboats? Where are they?"

"It ain't for me to say," Jenkins repeated, confused.

"Wake up Prine!" Mike snapped. "On the double!"

"Now I wouldn't like to do that," Jenkins stammered.

"I'll do it," Mike said. "Where's he quartered?"

Jenkins was overwhelmed by Mike's ferocity. He pointed weakly. "In the cottage at this end o' officer's row. But, if'n I was you I'd wait —"

He was talking to Mike's retreating back. Mike broke through the small group of troopers of the night guard that had gathered, and raced to the cottage Jenkins had indicated. It was one of the ugly, clapboard structures the army had built to house staff or married officers.

He mounted the small porch and pounded loudly on the door. "Prine!" he called. "Wake up! It's Mike McVey! Wake up! Are you there? Open this door! I've got to talk to you!"

"McVey?" Prine's angry voice was thick

with sleep. "What the hell are you doing here? Have you gone completely crazy?"

"Open up!" Mike demanded. "We've got to talk. I think that idiot, Cool, is going to put his foot into a trap. I just came from Cheyenne country."

The door opened. Prine stood in a long nightshirt, gripping a cocked Army pistol, which he raised. The hammer was eared back. "What are you up to, McVey?" he snarled. "You *have* turned Indian, haven't you? Everybody always knew that was your true color."

"Where's Cool gone with the outfit?" Mike demanded.

Prine glared. "What business is that of yours?"

"He hasn't gone across the river to try to rescue Nancy, has he?"

"If you're referring to poor Nancy Halstead, she's been given up as dead, thanks to your black friend. But we happen to know that he's alive, at least, and within reach. He's soon going to be made to pay for his crime."

"Then Cool *has* crossed the river!" Mike groaned. "On the steamboats, I take it? When did they pull out?"

"I see no reason to discuss military matters with you, McVey."

Mike grasped Prine by the front of his nightshirt. "Talk, man! They've got to be stopped! There still might be time!"

Prine swung the heavy barrel of the pistol in a blow that might have broken Mike's wrist, but he parried it with his free arm.

"Listen to me, Marsh!" he said, trying to speak calmly. "Nancy Halstead is alive and in a small village of Cheyenne that's being used to lure the colonel across the river. It's a trap and he's walking into it with the troops."

"The colonel knows what he's doing," Prine snapped. "He intends to teach these Indians a lesson and bring every one of them to the fort and hang them for what happened to Nancy. Our scouts have sighted this black man, Esau Solomon, with those Cheyenne."

"Nancy Halstead is with that village too," Mike said. "And so was I until last night, when I walked away. Didn't the scouts find that out too?"

"You're lying. Nancy Halstead is dead."

"She probably will be dead if Cool attacks that village — provided he gets even that far."

"What do you mean?"

"There are enough Cheyenne and Sioux warriors staked out across the river to eat

Cool and the outfit alive. I saw Sitting Bull and Crazy Horse of the Sioux holding pow-wow with the Cheyenne — saw them with my own eyes. Two Moons of the Cheyenne was there. Tribes as far away as the Ute country have sent in warriors. It isn't Cool who'll be teaching the lesson. Surely, his scouts warned him there were a lot of Indians in the country?"

"There were some reports of that," Prine said uneasily. "But they were following a great herd of buffalo."

"Bah!" Mike raged. "When did the troops pull out? Quit stalling."

Prine was cornered by Mike's vehemence. "Yesterday afternoon," he said reluctantly. "On the packets. The colonel intended to move up the river during the night, then land before daybreak a few miles below where this small village was last seen."

The packets would have followed the swing of the river well away from the route across country that Mike had traveled during the night. By this time, probably, the two companies of cavalry would be landing on the west side of the river.

Mike sagged a little. He had lost. The ghastly thought was in his mind that he should have stayed with Nancy. There might have been something he could have done.

But there was always hope. He still had to try to get back to her in time.

"I need a horse, Prine," he said.

"A horse? For what?"

"I've got to get there. She may still be alive. I might be able to help her."

He became aware that another person was in the unlighted room back of Marsh Prine. A woman in a dressing gown.

"Who's that?" Mike asked.

Prine again raised the cocked pistol. "Go back, Faith," he spoke to the woman. "This man is really insane. McVey, are you completely out of your senses? Are you trying to threaten my wife?"

"Your wife?"

In the faint light Mike saw now that she was the dark-haired girl who had been with Nancy when they had arrived at Fort Flagg the night that seemed so long ago.

"Of course it's my wife, you scoundrel, who else?"

"You didn't even wait to make sure Nancy was dead, did you Prine?" Mike asked. "You didn't even mourn her for long. You married another woman."

"What are you talking about?" Prine screeched. He raised his voice higher. "Sergeant! Sergeant-of-the-guard! This way! On the double!"

Jenkins and his squad of sentries had been waiting nearby. They came blundering out of the shadows.

"Arrest this lunatic!" Prine raged. "Throw him in the guardhouse. See to it that he stays there. I'll deal with him later."

His pistol was close to Mike, so close Mike seized it, blocking the hammer with his thumb. He wrested the weapon free and jammed its muzzle into Prine's belly. The girl in the background screamed in fear.

"I really wouldn't shoot him, ma'am," Mike told her. He addressed Jenkins. "I need a horse, Sergeant. Miss Halstead is alive. At least she was not many hours ago. I want to try to get to that Cheyenne village before Cool moves in. I want to warn him to turn back unless it's already too late, for I'm sure he's taking the outfit into an ambush."

Jenkins, caught between two fires, looked from Mike to Prine and back again. "Do what he says," Prine rasped. "Can't you see, he's out of his head? He's in a mood to kill me! Get him a horse if that's what he wants."

Jenkins and two enlisted men hurried away, heading toward the stables. Mike had a second thought. "Rig two horses," he shouted after them. "Bring a mount for Dr. Prine. He's going with me."

He added, "I'm sure you'd want to, if the command is in danger, wouldn't you, Marsh? And you owe it to Nancy to go with me this time. It was for you that she got into this thing, remember? Put on your clothes. Dress warm. We're riding."

He accompanied Prine to the bedroom and kept the pistol in his hand while the medic got into clothes and boots and pulled on an Army overcoat. His bride stood by, sobbing.

By the time Prine was ready, the horses had been brought up. "We could use a brace of carbines and another side gun, Jenkins," Mike said. "And about fifty rounds each. I'll carry the guns on my saddle until they're needed. And we could use a couple of blankets and some field rations if you can scare them up in a hurry. And I mean in a hurry."

Jenkins pointed to weapons and bedrolls on the saddles. "Already done so, sir," he said. "Figgered you'd need 'em if you was goin' acrost the river. Best of luck to you, sir. We'll all be hopin' the regiment don't git into nothin' it can't handle. I'm askin' to go along, with your permission. I guess I could round up about two squads to come along. That's about all. The colonel stripped down the garrison when he pulled out yesterday."

"One more wouldn't do much good,"

Mike said. "Better stay here, Jenkins. You might find yourself in hot enough water even back of these walls if the tribes decide to cross the river."

He prodded the two horses into motion, and he and Prine rode out of the stockade gate. Full, gray daylight lay over the land now. The first fires of morning were rising tiredly from the chimneys of Flagg City.

"I'll have that sergeant courtmartialed for this," Prine said between tight-set teeth. "As for you, McVey, you'll be lucky to escape the gallows. You were involved in kidnaping a woman. Now you've kidnaped a member of the military establishment, forced him to go with you against his will. The best you can hope for is to spend the rest of your life in prison."

Mike said nothing. He kept the horses at a full gallop, heading over the trail that led to Esau's place. He was remembering Esau's flatboat, for he believed the river would be too high to swim, and certainly there would be little chance of getting Prine and the horses across by that method.

He recalled that Esau's boat had been moored with a long painter. He hoped that the craft would still be afloat despite the rise in the river. His hope was fulfilled. The flat-boat was at its mooring, although it had been jammed into the brush and was in danger of being crushed by driftwood. It was also waterlogged by rain after so many days of inattention, and little more than its combing was showing.

"Help me!" Mike said. Freeing the painter, he waded into the river and floated the boat to shallower water where he could handle it more easily. He began rocking the boat to spill water from it. Shoving the craft aground, he raced out of the river and across the flat to Esau's cabin were he delved among the debris until he found a kettle that was intact enough to serve for bailing. He hurried back to the flatboat and began frantically bailing. He again called to Prine for assistance.

Prine remained in the saddle. "Do you actually intend to try to cross the river in that tub, McVey?" he demanded. "And do you actually believe what you've been telling me? You must have dreamed all this, especially the part about Nancy being alive and being used to lure the colonel into a trap."

"Get hold of this thing and help me drag its prow farther up on bank," Mike panted. "That'll drain the water out faster."

He put his shoulder to the task, pushing the laden boat higher on the shore. Water sluiced over the combing in a wave, blinding him. When his vision cleared, Marsh Prine wasn't there any longer. He heard the thud of receding hoofs. Prine was riding away, heading in the direction of Fort Flagg. He was taking Mike's mount with him.

Chapter 10

Mike drained the flatboat, but Prine's desertion lengthened the task and took that much more toll of his own endurance. It also increased the hazard of crossing the river single-handed. Mike hunted for the oars, but finally gave it up, deciding they must have burned along with Esau's other possessions.

He searched among the driftwood until he found a stout tree limb of the right length that might serve as a clumsy paddle. Except for the Army pistol, which had five shells in its chamber, he was unarmed, now that Prine had ridden away with the rifle. Also gone was the blanket Jenkins had rounded up to help shelter him from the cold.

He pushed the flatboat away from shore and scrambled aboard. The craft spun crazily when he began wielding the tree limb. He managed to steady it on its course after a period of practice. Flailing away, he continued to improve in his sculling until he could keep the prow pointed steadily across the current toward the distant shore.

He finally made it, but he knew he had

lost at least half a mile of distance down-stream. He staggered ashore and moored the boat. He was so spent he could only slog heavily along for a long time before his laboring lungs revived.

A thin sun formed a faint disk in the overcast, but that was enough to give him a bearing so that he could set a course that would bring him back to the river a distance to the north.

Noon came, and the day began to fade into a cheerless afternoon. The overcast deepened. He had lost all track of time and distance. He was moving like a ghost, his teeth bared with the effort, his eyes blood-shot and glazed.

He had not realized how far along was the afternoon when he heard the guns. Their stuttering was faint and far away. It was like the crackle of dry cottonwood that had been fed to a fire. But he had heard such sounds before and there was no mistaking them.

The stuttering faded as the wind shifted. His straining ears caught only the sluffing of his dragging feet. Then it came again and grew distinct. He found himself running, prodded into new strength. The volume of rifle fire increased. It grew to angry, ominous snarling somewhere in the plains.

Again, Mike knew from experience what he was hearing. Those first, intermittent thuds had been the initial meeting of the skirmishers. Now, all the combatants had come into action. The roar reached a sustained note as though a peal of thunder was being echoed and reechoed by the clouds.

It came from the north and slightly east. He swerved in that direction. He began keeping to what cover he could find. The plain around him was devoid of human life, but jackrabbits were bouncing past, ears flattened, and quail, sagehens and other fowl were roaring by on the wing. All wildlife was fleeing from that deep mechanical voice that raged in the distance.

A deeper, bronze voice assailed Mike's ears — the heavy report of a howitzer. It bellowed again and again. In the past, Mike had stated at inquiries into unsuccessful campaigns against the tribes in the Platte Valley that the presence of wheeled artillery had been a great handicap to cavalry units which must depend on mobility to match that of their foes in fighting the horse Indians of the plains.

Roscoe Cool, in love with the panoply and age-old routine of war, had taken howitzers across the river and was using them against mounted men that were targets as elusive as the antelope that Mike sighted fleeing into the depths of the land.

Mike followed the broken line of a shallow wash, floundering to his knees in water. The gully widened, and he saw the wide expanse of the Missouri ahead, into which it emptied. He had crossed the neck of the bow and was back at the river.

Then he came upon the flat where Cool and the regiment had come ashore from the packets. The wheel marks of the howitzers and their carriages were deep in the rain-softened soil. Cool had brought three pieces.

Mike could trace it all. Here was where the sergeants had mustered the files, and there was where the ranks had fallen into route order by squads. They had set out with pennants flying, no doubt, and Cool giving orders to the buglers. He might even have brought the post band along.

There was no sign of the steamboats, other than the marks of the gangplanks, and no way of telling whether they had withdrawn upstream or down.

Mike followed the broad swath of tracks made by the cavalry horses. They had headed north, keeping the Missouri on their right flank. They had moved less than half a mile when the fight had started.

The battle evidently was receding northward, as though one side was retreating — retreating fast. The thud of howitzers had ended. He came upon a dead cavalry horse. It had two arrows in its flank. A trooper's boot was wedged in a stirrup. Farther on, lay the rider himself. He had been speared in the back. This was where the skirmishers of the opposing sides had first met. The torn headdress of a warrior fluttered in the wind from a clump of brush. The dead soldier had not been mutilated. Evidently the slayers had been driven off by the other troopers, but they had not been given the chance to take their comrade's body with them.

That was only the beginning. It was like fitting together the parts of a jigsaw puzzle — a tragic puzzle whose pieces formed a bitter pattern. Farther along lay two more dead horses. Also a carbine with a shattered stock, a broken saber, discarded haversacks, empty rifle shells and campaign hats. Two dead Indian ponies lay in a swale, and arrows jutted here and there from the soil. Here was where the first pony charge had been met and beaten. Clouds of flies hovered over dark, crimson stains in the grass.

There had been a short, sharp fight here, some of it hand-to-hand, and the battle had moved along northward. Crows, magpies were overhead. A dark mound turned out to be that of an Indian pony with a warrior crushed and dead beneath it. He was a Sioux and had been hit in the face by a Springfield bullet which had ranged upward, emerging through a large hole torn out of the back of the skull.

More debris scattered the plain ahead, but the majority of the dead had been carried away by both sides. Mike followed this grim trail, with the gunfire an increasing thunder ahead. The sound rose and fell. At times it would still almost entirely. Then it would resume and swell until it became a steady peal. Then it would die only to spring to savage life again.

He came upon the howitzers. They had been spiked, the caissons blown up, and the horses slaughtered. He could see that from this point on it had no longer been a retreat, but a desperate flight by men who had realized they were facing impossible odds. Bodies of both troopers and Indians began to dot the plain.

Apparently the companies had managed to maintain a semblance of discipline and cohesion and had been able to take their wounded with them rather than leave them to torture, but they had been forced to abandon their dead. Mike began seeing familiar faces of men who had served under him and now lay in the grotesque postures of violent death.

Empty rifle and pistol shells caught the glint of the pale sun. Arrows littered the land, and this was further proof of how savage had been the fight and how it had moved along at a pace a horse could gallop. Arrows were valuable munition that could be salvaged, but the warriors had not taken time to replenish their quivers, so fierce had been the pursuit. That would be the task of squaws and children later on. Mike became aware of this danger, realizing that the salvage crew would soon be appearing on the battlefield which still remained vacant except for the dead.

He reached the crest of a rise, and for the first time saw the battle itself, and its scope. To the right, curving northwesterly and vanishing into the mauve mists of the waning day was the Missouri River.

Some distance ahead — nearly a mile — Cool's command was pinned down on a tongue of land that jutted from the inner shore of the bend in the river. It was surrounded on three sides by water and connected to land by a narrow neck of dry terrain that appeared to be facing inundation by the rising river. In fact, Mike could see that the entire tongue might be covered by the river within hours.

The cavalry men had been wedged into this trap by overwhelming numbers. The entire area was alive with motion and color. Gunfire flashed wickedly from a small wooded ridge that commanded the tongue of land, though at long range. Indian marksmen were hidden there, pouring rifle fire into the position of the trapped troopers. The cavalrymen had abandoned their horses, which stood pathetically between the lines, the Indians unwilling to pay the price that would be exacted for rounding them up.

Farther back, hundreds of other Indians waited in semi-military formations. Some were mounted, evidently prepared to charge the semi-island when the word came from the strategists who were directing the allied tribes. Other groups were on foot and were evidently being held to follow the mounted groups when the charge was ordered.

Still farther from the battlefield, campfires were being lighted. Lodges were being pitched. Scores of them. Hundreds of them. The squaws had arrived, and food and shelter was being prepared for the warriors who had been fighting the greater part of the day in the long pursuit of the retreating quarry. The tribes were preparing for a long fight, if necessary.

Through all that long, grim trail there had been one name in Mike's mind. Nancy!

He kept refusing to let himself think about the very thing he had said might happen. White captives were usually killed when the army attacked a village. He had said that awful thing. It had been true in the past too many times.

He peered with eyes crimson with strain and fatigue. Never before had the Indians shown such unity, such power, such concerted strength. There was no way of estimating their numbers. The cookfires began to speckle the plain as far as his eye could carry. Great herds of ponies were being held on grazing in the distance.

A lull had come in the gunfire. That ended in a new burst of fury. The pony charge had been ordered. Hundreds of mounted warriors burst from hiding in a long line, and raced toward the tongue of land, screeching and shooting.

The besieged troopers had one item in their favor. Their position was littered with driftwood and thick with scrub willows. The trunks of several sizable trees had been lodged there by floods in the past, and these afforded natural breastworks. They had the river at their back and on the flanks, and while they could not retreat, they could not be surrounded.

Their position remained silent as the charge came thundering upon them. Then someone gave the order and the Springfields opened up. Either Roscoe Cool was gaining in experience, or, more likely, Major Bill Stevens, a veteran officer who had seen much fighting both on the plains and in the Civil War, was giving the orders.

Ponies piled up, warriors were torn from their foot-straps to fall limply to the ground or be dragged. The Indians reached the swampy backwater on the flanks of the tongue of land, and foam flew as the ponies thrashed and floundered in the muck.

They could not sustain the charge, or absorb the losses the yellowlegs were exacting. The charge crested a score of yards from the front line of the defenders. It reeled back and broke. The majority of them were Sioux, Mike believed. He picked out one that might have been Crazy Horse himself, trying to rally them. But even the inspirational war chief could not convince them that they could prevail. The survivors streamed out of range, carrying their dead and wounded with them.

Mike continued to scan the vast, scattered encampment, studying it section by section. The Indians fought under the direction of one leader, evidently, or perhaps a council of chiefs, but they were maintaining their separate tribal and village identities in the camp. The lodges stood in groups apart from the others. There were many large villages on the plain, but it was the smaller groups that Mike inspected with feverish hope.

He discarded them, one by one. None was as small as had been the one Gray Buffalo had led in his wandering attempt to lure the regiment to this side of the river.

Dusk was deepening fast. It was evident the fighting was over for the day at least. The soldiers, hemmed in, could not escape, and the tribes could starve them out at their leisure if they chose.

It had been a long and exhausting day for both red and white combatants. Dead and wounded were still being brought in from the battlefield by the Indians. In the failing light, Mike's eyes began to follow a big man in Indian garb, whom he had not observed before. The man was Esau.

Esau was on foot and was carrying a wounded or dead Cheyenne in his arms. Mike desperately tried to keep track of the big man as he made his way through the labyrinth of the encampment where Indians were moving in all directions like a disturbed ant heap.

Council fires were built and scalp dancing was already being started. Squaws were beginning their lamentations for sons and husbands who would enter their lodges no more. Coups were being counted.

A solemn war council was under way at a medicine pole which had been erected almost in the center of the great carpet of tribal units. A large fire blazed there. Medicine men were tossing powder into the flames which shot up tongues of colored smoke. Important chiefs were gathering, some still in battle paint and breechclouts, some in full ceremonial dress.

Mike lost sight of Esau and his heart sank. He rose to his feet, risking danger of being sighted. It seemed hours to him, though it was only a minute or two, and he had been on the point of giving up, when he spotted the big man once more. This time he discovered Esau's destination. Partly hidden by a larger collection of lodges in the foreground was a group of a dozen lodges — a unit that had become familiar to Mike in the past. It was Gray Buffalo's village, apparently still intact. It had been given a place of some honor in the general scheme of the encampment, for it stood within sight of where the chiefs were gathering for their council of war.

Esau entered this smaller village, carrying his burden. Then Mike's heart leaped mightily. Two persons in Indian female grab came to meet him. They took the burden from him and carried it into Gray Buffalo's lodge. Mike's heart sank, for he was sure they were Elk Woman and Snow Dove. He had hoped against hope that one might be Nancy.

He decided that the burden Esau had brought in from the battlefield was Gray Buffalo, either wounded or dead. He crouched down, watching, but now it was all fading back of the curtain that night was lowering. There were only the council fires and the shadows dancing and the medley of exultant shouting from warriors who leaped and cavorted and boasted of their prowess during the fight. This, and the undertone of the mourning for the dead by the squaws. The drums were sounding in many places. All this combined in a throbbing, wild pulsebeat.

An occasional rifleshot broke from the river battlefield where the trap was being kept tightly closed. The guns of the troopers remained mainly silent. They did not dare build a cookfire that would silhouette them as targets.

Mike forced himself to wait until darkness had settled. He must work his way through the heart of the great encampment to Gray Buffalo's village. Hundreds of Indians still moved about, visiting from fire to fire, reveling in that ultimate excitement that only men who risk their lives in battle know. Today they had fought and were still alive. Tomorrow they would fight again and tomorrow they might be riding the Great Medicine Road into the sky. Tonight they were alive and frenzied with the lust of battle, and the fascination of it.

He took stock of his chances. His skin was darkened by sun and exposure so that he might pass, with luck, without being challenged on that score. Darkness and the swirling excitement in the encampment would be his biggest allies.

He arose and walked boldly across the battlefield and into the encampment. Its enormous size was an additional aid to him. The Indians were inspired by the belief they were about to deal the yellowlegs a blow that would break their spirit and drive them forever from their hunting grounds. When the sun came up again, the troopers would live their last day and the word would go back to that mysterious Great Father in a place called Washington that the red man was still supreme in his own domain.

And so, on this night, the Cheyenne and Sioux, the Arapaho and Crow, the Ute and Shoshone, were dancing and calling each their brothers. The wailing of the squaws was a lost note in the wild oratory and boasting that was going on around the fires. The thud of coup sticks on council poles echoed across the plains. Dancers leaped insanely, brandishing weapons and telling the story of their bravery in the fight. Some waved the scalps of fallen soldiers.

Mike walked without haste, and the Indians who crossed his path did not give him a second glance. Their attention was on the dancers and not on the muffled figure that passed by. He continued to move casually, pretending also to be fascinated by the scenes at the council fires.

He came at last near the big council fire where a chief with great oratorical powers was making a long speech. He was telling the others that on the morrow the yellow-legs must be annihilated.

Mike moved out of range of his voice and approached the smaller group of lodges. A fire was burning in Gray Buffalo's lodge, but the remainder of the village had been deserted in favor of attendance at the council gatherings.

Mike could hear the rattles and bells of a medicine man sounding in Gray Buffalo's lodge. A massive figure suddenly stepped from darkness and blocked Mike's path. He started to snatch the six-shooter from his belt, but a powerful hand seized his wrist.

"No, Mike," Esau's deep voice murmured. "We're still friends."

"Yes," Mike said. "I hope so."

"I been waitin', watchin' fer you," Esau said. "I knowed you'd try to come back."

"Then you know *why* I came back."

"I know. You come lookin' fer her, fer Missy Halstead."

Mike had to force his lips to frame the next question. "Is she — is she — ?"

"She still alive," Esau said. "Leastwise I think so, an' pray she is."

"Aren't you sure?"

"De squaws come to kill her dis mawnin' after dey found out dat Runnin' Wolf had gone under."

"Running Wolf? Who's he?"

"A Cheyenne chief from another village what offered Gray Buffalo ten ponies yesterday if he could take Missy Halstead as his squaw. Runnin' Wolf was a war chief, what sat in council wid chief like Gall an' Two Moons. He was one o' de first to be killed by de calv'ry when de fight started this mawnin'."

"But they didn't kill her?"

"Snow Dove fought dem squaws off. Her father came ridin' up an' chased dem back to dar own villages. He say Missy Nancy will still be de wife of a warrior an' be a Cheyenne woman. But now Gray Buffalo is done fer, hisself. He still alive, but he's goin' to de Great Spirit. He got a bullet through de lungs. I brung him in from de battlefield myself. I don' wan him to die. He de father o' Ruth. He be good to a black man like me. Now he goin' to ride in de sky. De medicine man know it too. Hear dem rattles? Dey only sound 'em slow like dat when a Cheyenne is dyin'."

"What about Nancy if he dies?"

"I don' reckon even Snow Dove kin save her. Seems like a witch doctor warned Runnin' Wolf dat he'd never live through de fight if'n he went through wid his notion o' buyin' a white squaw. Dat same witch doctor said dar would be death in Gray Buffalo's lodge too, 'less he got rid o' de one dat was puttin' a curse on it. Looks like de witch doctor man was right. Runnin' Wolf already dead. Gray Buffalo is dyin'."

Mike peered close at Esau. "You don't believe in witch doctors, Esau. Your faith is in the Good Book."

"I don' know what to believe," Esau said doggedly. "All I know is dat what the witch man said has come true."

"Men get killed in battle," Mike said. "And a lot more will go under. Do you know what's happening out there, Esau?"

"I know," Esau said grimly. "De regiment is done fer. Dey'll be wiped out tomorrow. De river's still risin'. Dat place they're holdin' out on will be under water by tomorrow night. Dey'll be killed or drowned. Colonel Cool thought he was goin' to gobble up this little village like you'd swat a 'skeeter. 'Stead, he found hisself in big trouble."

The shadows had suddenly stopped moving in Gray Buffalo's lodge. The medicine man's rattles were silenced. Then the voices of Elk Woman and Snow Dove began to rise in the doleful dirge of mourning. Gray Buffalo was dead.

Chapter 11

The medicine man emerged from the lodge and disappeared into the darkness, fearful that Gray Buffalo's relatives might hold him accountable for failure to ward off the demon of death.

Mike ran to the lodge. Esau pursued him, pleading with him to stop, but Mike tore free from the black man's restraining hand and entered.

Elk Woman and Snow Dove were rocking back and forth on their knees beside the blanket-covered body of the chief, sounding their lament of grief. Elk Woman was already gashing her breast and fingers with a knife. Both she and the young girl had the fixed, trancelike stare of utter grief, and seemed unaware that Mike had entered.

Nancy lay bound hand and foot on a robe. She looked up with eyes that once again held the deep, dark resignation to death, the same look he had seen in her the night he had talked her out of using the knife on herself.

Now, once again, he saw life and hope return in her, saw a vast, wild joy and a tenderness so boundless he stood humbled. She kept trying to say his name as he found a knife and cut the rawhide bonds. The words would not come.

She was unable to rise, for the thongs had numbed her wrists and ankles. Mike lifted her in his arms. He slashed a slit in the rear wall of the lodge and prepared to carry her with him into the darkness.

Esau had entered the lodge. "Come with us," Mike said to him. "You don't really belong here."

The black man was torn by conflict. He looked at Snow Dove, and the Cheyenne girl seemed to understand his travail. She halted her mourning. She embraced her mother, then came to Esau's side and slid a hand into his massive palm.

"If you stay, Man-of-the-Night," Snow Dove said, "you will die. My people do not believe you have become a Cheyenne. They think that some day you might turn against them. And I think there is a curse on any man who lives in this lodge. And any woman. I wish to go with you."

The conflict faded in Esau's face. A peace came. He and Snow Dove moved across the lodge and joined Mike. The four of them crept out into the night away from where Elk Woman still mourned the dead chief.

"No talk," Mike warned. "Some of them might hear. And walk slowly. We don't want to attract attention."

The dancing and coup-counting had reached a frenzy in the great encampment. The area was bedlam. From a distance, gunshots still sounded at intervals, marking the battleground where the soldiers were held besieged.

Nancy said she could walk, and Mike set her on her own feet and supported her until she had steadied. They kept working their way toward the outer rim of the camp, avoiding the glow of the council fires, circling the hazardous points.

Their luck had held so long that Mike was beginning to breathe a little easier. The campfires were fewer ahead, and he could see the blackness of the empty plain offering further safety beyond. The intermittent rifle fire was growing fainter. Another few minutes and they would be in the clear.

It was an Indian dog that discovered them. The animal charged from a lodge, sounding its shrill, screaming alarm. It happened so suddenly that Nancy uttered her first sound, a low, terrified scream.

That brought an Indian woman, who had evidently returned to her lodge from the festivities on some errand. She came hurrying and was abruptly face-to-face with Mike and Nancy.

She was a heavy woman, with hair in a single braid. She stood, amazed, for an instant. Then she wheeled and began running away on her short legs. She screeched an alarm. The dog, slinking into the shadows, continued to yammer shrilly.

Mike snatched up a clod and hurled it. That rid them of the dog, at least, for the animal uttered a yelp of dismay and took to its heels.

"Run!" Mike snapped.

Nancy was not yet up to that, so he picked her up bodily. Esau had his hand on Snow Dove's arm and almost lifted her off her feet as he raced with her.

Behind them, the squaw was still screaming the alarm, but the lodges in that area were deserted, their occupants having gathered at the council fires. The woman's voice receded as she ran farther to summon help.

Mike was forced to place Nancy on her feet again. He was nearing the end of his endurance. "Snow Dove should go back," he told Esau. "She can't leave her people."

"No, no, no!" the Cheyenne girl protested. She moved closer to Esau. "I will stay with him."

They heard the stir of ponies in the darkness ahead. A dozen or more animals were held on picket for emergency use, evidently, for they were equipped with pad saddles, halters and foot slings.

"Can you hang onto a horse?" Mike asked Nancy.

"Of course," she said. "I've done some riding back home. I could hang onto a tiger if necessary tonight."

Mike and Esau moved among the picketed animals and seized the four that were easiest to control. They freed the others and stampeded them away into the night. The mounts they had selected fought for a time, terrorized by the scent of an alien race, but finally quieted.

Sounds in the encampment told that pursuit was forming. Mike and Esau lifted the girls on ponies and swung onto the other mounts. They all clung to manes and circingles as the animals bolted away.

For a time all they could do was to let the mounts run. Mike's pony stumbled over some obstruction in the darkness and slid on its knees for yards, but managed to regain its feet and race ahead again, apparently unhurt.

He believed the animals were heading down the river, but he and Esau were unable to control direction and had to trust to luck.

By instinct, the ponies clung together in their stampede. The clatter of their hoofs wiped out all other sound, and there was no telling if pursuit was an immediate danger.

Esau's mount fell, turning head-over-heels. The big man managed to plunge clear so that he was not caught beneath the animal. Mike and the girls yanked their ponies to a halt.

Esau was back on his feet. "I'm all right," he panted, "but dat pony's a goner. I heered his neck bust, or maybe it was his backbone."

They could hear riders in the distance, but there was no way of telling whether the pursuers had found their trail. The glow of the fires in the great tribal camp hung sullenly in the sky, now well back of them.

Because of Esau's weight, they shifted Snow Dove to the pony with Nancy to ride double, while the black man mounted the third animal. They kicked the mounts into motion again, but the ponies had spent their strength in that wild race and were now only able to proceed at a trot.

"Where do you suppose we are?" Mike asked.

"River kain't be fur away," Esau said. "I kin smell it. It's got to be off'n to our left."

They swerved in that direction. Within

minutes they emerged in sight of the dark Missouri. The river now occupied its entire flood channel, sweeping by a broad flood, and was beginning to invade the plain itself at points where the banks were low.

The great stream was baring its teeth. Somewhere in the darkness it was growling and grinding as though an animal was rending flesh. Near at hand, it hissed and muttered as it swirled past. Whorls of foam rose to the surface, catching the distant, saffron reflection of the glow from the Indian camp. These would break in spurts of spray, then vanish to be replaced by others.

"Listen!" Nancy breathed.

The voice of the river had hidden the sound of approaching ponies. Pursuers were near. They lashed their mounts into a gallop again. The animals splashed across a flat that was being invaded by the river. A clump of brush stood above water on a small rise. They halted the ponies and dismounted in that shelter.

Mike moved away from the sound of the labored breathing of the animals and listened. He made out only faint, distant sounds. He decided their pursuers had veered off on some false scent and were west of them.

He returned to his companions. "We

234

better stay here for a while, at least," he said.

"Kain't stay too long," Esau said. "Dey'll circle back, figgerin' dey got us pinned ag'in de river, jes like dey got de regiment in a bind today."

Nancy leaned wearily against Mike. "I never expected to see you again," she said. "I still can't believe it's actually you. Are you really here? Am I dead, and is all this what you see when you go up the Great Medicine Road? Do you see only the happy things you wanted to see in life?"

"Happy things?"

"What else could this be? They were going to kill me. I knew that. Snow Dove saved me once. She couldn't have stopped them again. Not after Gray Buffalo died. And after Running Wolf was killed. Even the squaws who had become friendly suddenly wanted to do away with me. I was afraid even of Elk Woman. I would not have lived through the night."

She stood on tiptoe, drew his face down and kissed him on the lips. "I am sorry you came back," she said. "I always believed that you would. I think that's what kept me alive. I had a knife hidden and I intended to use it if you did not, but I prayed you'd return. That was a terrible thing to do."

"Terrible thing?"

"I must be a hoodoo. First Running Wolf, then Gray Buffalo. Now I've brought you to death's door. Esau was trying to tell us that we haven't got much chance. They'll surround us before daybreak. Why did you throw away your life, McVey?"

"You know the answer to that," Mike said, almost angrily.

"Tell me. Tell me yourself. I want to hear it."

"For the same reason you wouldn't let Esau kill the man you were going to marry. The man you love."

"The man I love?"

"You do love Marsh Prine, don't you? You're not the kind to marry a man for any other reason."

She spoke to the black man. "Esau, that night you came to Fort Flagg and I went away with you did you really think — ?"

Mike whispered abruptly, "Quiet!"

They stood frozen, listening to the splashing of hoofs in the flooded field nearby. The sound passed well off to their right. In the darkness they were unable to tell the exact number of riders, but Mike believed there must have been nearly a score of them. They heard other distant sounds. The pursuit was gathering. But silence eventually came again. Mike surmised that the Indians had not realized how close they had been to their quarry and had been merely taking a short cut across the shallow backwater to higher ground beyond.

"We better move along," he said.

"What you got in mind?" Esau asked. "If'n we go fussin' around we might blunder into some o' dem Cheyenne an' Sioux. We kain't swim de rivah. Too high."

"Your flatboat is on this side," Mike said. "I brought it across. It's a long way from here but we ought to be able to reach it before daybreak."

"Den what?"

"Try to do something for those men back there."

"Ain't nothin' nobody kin do. Not less dar's a miracle. I don' reckon dar's enough soldiers left at de fo't to be of any help."

"What about the steamboats?" Mike said. "Where are they?"

"Kain't say. De Injuns waited 'til de steamboats had landed all de yallalegs, den moved in. De steamboats went back down de rivah. Maybe dey are back at de fo't, waitin' orders." He added, "I reckon dey'll wait a long time."

They mounted and urged the unwilling ponies ahead. They rode in silence, fearing that even a whisper might reach an enemy's ears. At intervals Mike would call a halt and they would listen, conning the night for information. They occasionally heard rumors of pursuit in the distance but none near enough to threaten them.

"It looks like we've shaken them off," Mike said.

" 'Til mornin', maybe," Esau said.

"It could be they figure it isn't worth it," Mike said. "They've got bigger game in sight tomorrow and they all will want to be on hand."

Nancy spoke. "You were talking a while ago about the man I was going to marry, McVey. I've been waiting a chance to discuss this with you."

"What's there to discuss?" Mike asked.

"Should we take Marsh Prine as the subject, for instance?"

"Who else?" Mike said. "If you're worried about him, I can assure you he's at the fort and should be safe and sound and in good health. In fact, I talked to him there."

"That's nice," she said. "Very nice. I'm happy to know about his health. Why isn't he with the regiment?"

"Cool left him at the fort and took two shavetail surgeons with him. Marsh Prine is lucky in more ways than one."

"I've heard you mention Marsh Prine's

luck before," she said. She seemed angry about something. "I'm happy that he isn't back there with the regiment. I'd be still happier if I knew that you and Esau and Snow Dove were as safe as he seems to be."

Mike leaned from his pony, peering close in the darkness, trying to read her expression. "I don't understand you," he said.

"I understand one thing about you, McVey," she said, "which is that you are a thick-skulled, bumble-headed idiot, that you make me so angry I could slap you! That — !"

"Please, missy," Esau groaned. "Don' talk so loud."

Nancy yanked her pony away from Mike's side and joined Snow Dove. The two of them rode along, and Mike heard them whispering in a mixture of Cheyenne and English. They began giggling, apparently enjoying some secret.

"Dis is no time fer dat sort o' thing either," Esau told them in a massive, disapproving whisper. "We ain't out o' de woods yet by a long shot."

Daybreak was near when Mike abruptly called a halt. "Listen!" he breathed.

They sat rigid, trying to quiet the ponies. "Do you hear it?" he murmured.

"What is it, Mike?" Esau asked.

"Steamboat engine," Mike said. "And not too far away."

They excitedly kicked the ponies into motion, swinging toward the river which lay somewhere west of them. They found that they had to make their way through a half-mile of swampy water and brush in which driftwood from past floods had lodged. They were finally forced to dismount and lead the ponies. Twice, they were compelled to backtrack and make tedious, circuitous routes to avoid impassable stretches.

Whenever they paused to listen, Mike expected the sound of the steamboat engine to have faded upriver or down. But it still remained in their ears, faint but constant.

Full daylight lay over the land when they found their way at last, mud-coated, to a sandbar into full view of the main river. A packet, its paddlewheel turning slowly, lay in midstream. It was the *Far Frontier*. At first she appeared deserted. Then Mike saw that someone was at the wheel in the pilothouse. Only the man's head was visible above the boiler plate with which the wheel house was lined shoulder-high. A firebox door opened in the boiler room giving forth a ruddy glow on the lower deck.

The packet had put out a bow anchor upstream which held it in position in the broad river. The paddlewheel was revolving at slow speed in order to help offset the drag of the craft against the anchor and to give it steerageway so that it would not swing toward either shore.

The firebox door clanged. Fuel had been fed to the boilers to maintain steam. Too much steam, in fact, for a safety valve popped, emitting a rush of steam with a roar that brought startled little screams from both Nancy and Snow Dove. The Cheyenne girl started to scurry to hiding in the brush, then paused and stared in awe.

The valve closed, the roar ended. Someone lifted a voice aboard the packet. "Look! Thar, on thet sandbar! Injuns! A whole pack of 'em. They're comin' at us!"

Before Mike realized their danger, rifles opened up from bulwarks on the hurricane deck. The *Far Frontier* was a long way from being deserted. Men had been crouching back of the barriers, with rifles ready.

"Down!" Mike shouted, and hurled himself at Nancy, toppling her to the ground and shielding her with his own body. A bullet smashed through a bush a few feet from them.

Grasping her in his arms, he rolled into the shelter of a driftwood log. "You fools!"

he yelled. "Hold your fire! We're not Indians! We're friends!"

Esau had attempted to protect Snow Dove in the same manner, but the big man had slipped in the muddy underfooting and had fallen. Several rifles were still in action on the packet. They were using Henrys or Winchesters, evidently.

A slug ricocheted from the river a dozen feet from Esau. It screeched by with a wicked buzz. Another tore into the sand within inches of the black man.

Snow Dove leaped in, screaming wildly in Cheyenne, and placed her own small body as a shield. "No, honey!" Esau gasped. "No. Get back! Get — !"

Mike heard the mushy, sickening impact as a bullet tore through flesh. Snow Dove uttered a gasp and fell back, a numbed, startled look in her face. Esau crouched above her, gazing at the blood that stained the Cheyenne girl's smock.

Chapter 12

Nancy tore free of Mike's grasp and crawled to the side of the Indian girl. She cut open Snow Dove's smock, baring the wound. The bullet had gone through bone and flesh below the right shoulder joint.

The rifles on the packet had been emptied. Mike could hear the sounds of frantic hands reloading. "Injuns!" the first voice kept screeching. "They're goin' to try to board us!"

Mike arose and ran to the river's edge. He tore off his headband. "You double-cursed fools!" he yelled. "This is Mike McVey! We've got Miss Halstead with us! Alive! There's a Cheyenne girl with us, but she's one of us! You've shot her! Hold your fire before you murder more of us!"

There was a long silence aboard the packet. Presently heads arose and eyes made a cautious appraisal of the shore.

"Are you aboard, Flannery?" Mike yelled.

A shadow in the pilothouse turned into the head and bull shoulders of Pat Flannery, captain of the *Far Frontier*. He opened a slide window and spoke over the top of the iron shield. "Is that really you, McVey?"

"Of course it is!" Mike replied. "Tell those idiots to stop shooting at us. They've already maybe killed a girl."

"Don't believe him, Cap'n," a voice croaked from among the riflemen. "It's a trap. He's only tryin' to git us skelped. Likely thar's a hundred Injuns hid out there back o' him."

Nancy raised her voice. "I'm Nancy Halstead! We've got a wounded girl here, shot by you confounded people! What in blazes are you doing here anyway, with the regiment being massacred by thousands of Indians not far from here?"

Again there was instant silence. A reflection blinked from the packet. Mike saw that Flannery was using field glasses, scanning the shore.

"Massacred?" Flannery's voice had suddenly lost its bull-like quality. Evidently he had identified both Nancy and Mike and Esau and had found no evidence of a trap.

"Send a boat ashore for us," Mike yelled. "Hurry! There are Indians around. They hunted us all night. They might show up."

"Don't listen to him, Cap'n," the frightened voice pleaded again from a lower deck. "He's lyin'. He's turned Injun. Look at him!

He's wearin' Injun clothes, an' so air all the rest o' them. An' thar's thet nigger thet stole Miss Halstead. They're makin' her say what she said."

Flannery continued to hesitate. "I'm swimming aboard, Flannery," Mike yelled. "If I'm lying, I'll be the first one you can kill."

A distance upstream, the shore curved so that a tongue of land lay almost directly above the position of the packet. Mike splashed and floundered along the shore until he reached the point, then waded in and began swimming. The current carried him swiftly down upon the steamboat. It nearly carried him past, for the eyes and faces that looked down on him from over the barricades seemed blankly unable to comprehend his need, and none moved to toss him a line. Then Pat Flannery, himself, cursing the stupidity of his crew, came thundering down from the pilothouse to the lower deck, seized a line and hurled its end in time for Mike to grasp it. Clinging to it with his last strength, he was hauled aboard.

"A fine fish I've caught," Flannery said.

Mike found himself looking into the bores of rifles. Flannery was backed by half a dozen men, some of whom were members of the crew and others cavalrymen.

"Send the skiff ashore for the others, Flannery!" Mike croaked. "Hurry! Don't you understand? The regiment is surrounded up the river. They've got the whole Cheyenne and Sioux nations against them. They can't last through the day. They might already have gone under."

Flannery studied him for a moment. Then he forcibly shoved two of the crewmen toward a skiff that stood on the lower deck for emergency use. "Git movin'!" he snapped. "McVey must be tellin' the truth. He knows I'd like nothin' better than to string him up if he wasn't. Row like you never rowed before. Fetch them three aboard. An' be mighty certain the Halstead gal gits here safe."

The skiff was swiftly launched, with the two rivermen bending their backs to the oars.

"Where's the other steamboat?" Mike asked. "The *Far West*?"

"Back at the fort," Flannery said. "Fer repairs. Boiler head blew. An' what's this about the regiment bein' in trouble?"

"Trouble? It's a lot worse than that. And why haven't you heard about it?"

"I ain't heerd a word from the colonel since me an' the *Far West* landed him an' the rigiment acrost the river yesterday mornin'."

He was bent on pickin' up a small village o' Cheyenne the scouts had reported. The black man had been seen wid this bunch, an' the colonel figured on makin' him pay for stealin' the Halstead gal. Everybody had give her up as dead."

"What are you doing here, lying in the river?"

"Colonel's orders. He was afeared the Injuns would see or hear the steamboats an' clear out if we went any further up the river. He wanted to slip up on them at daybreak an' surround 'em. He told us to lay to in the river 'til he sent word where we was to pick up the regiment. The *Far West* had this boiler trouble an' Cap'n Bixby decided to go back to Flagg where he'd have better means o' repair in a hurry!"

The skiff had reached shore, and Mike could see Snow Dove being lifted aboard. Nancy and Esau followed. The craft swung away at once, with the crewmen contesting the current.

"It's up to you, Flannery," Mike said. "One packet is better than none at all."

Flannery drew a long breath. "Is it that bad, McVey?"

"Can't I get it through your head that Cool's got himself in a tight fix? The regiment's up against half the Indians on the plains. Sitting Bull is in it. So is Crazy Horse, Two Moons and Gall. The outfit found themselves surrounded, instead of them surrounding the small village that was bait for Cool. They fought a running retreat for ten miles or more. They lost the howitzers and all their horses. They were hunkered in weeds and deadfalls on a small spit of land at dark last night with the river rising and sure to drown them out before long. They've already lost a lot of men. You've got to get this tub up there and get them off."

"How fur upriver is this place?"

"Fifteen miles at a guess. Maybe farther."

"Did ye see it? Describe the lay o' the land to me."

Mike did so as best he could, mentioning the wooded ridge that afforded cover to the Indians, and the tongue of land itself.

"I'm afeared I know the place very well," Flannery said grimly. "An' it's no place fer a packet. That west shore along there is nothin' but snags, rock chains an' swamps fer miles."

"And Indians?"

Flannery reddened. "You ain't tryin' to say that Pat Flannery's afraid, are you, McVey?"

"I'm saying you're showing yellow all the way up from your tailbone."

"For that I will beat ye to a pulp, McVey, when I have the time."

"That's a deal, Flannery. Right now, you're running this packet up there to take aboard the regiment — or what's left of it. Unless you get under way in a hell of a hurry, I'll see to it that you stand trial for cowardice and failure to perform your duty. As captain of a packet chartered to the Army, I believe you're given temporary rank as an Army officer and therefore subject to court-martial."

"McVey!" Flannery said, white-lipped. " 'Tis a dastardly thing to do to accuse me of bein' a coward. Ye know better. But, I warn ye that it will likely only mean loss of this packet. I would only put this boat onto a snag or a chain that would rip out its bottom. I know the river. You do not."

"I know something about the river too," Mike said. "It is high and still rising. They tell me that flatbottomed packets like this one can cross a cornfield on a heavy dew. The lives of three hundred men or more are in a jackpot up there. If you're afraid to try it, show me how to handle the wheel and I'll take it there myself. Esau Solomon can stoke the boilers. You and the rest of your crew can swim to shore if you want it that way."

He was bluffing and Flannery knew it. He was hitting Flannery at his weakest point — his Irish pride. The man was no coward. It was only that he could not visualize the real desperation of the regiment's situation.

He stood a moment, glaring at Mike, his big fists knotted, hungry to avenge the aspersion on his courage. "Later, an' that's a sacred promise, McVey," he raged. "It will be hard to wait. Then I will smash you as I would a mosquito. But this is not the time."

The skiff swung alongside, and crewmen held it against the current. Esau stepped aboard, carrying Snow Dove in his arms. Nancy followed.

Tears were streaking down Esau's face. "She's gone," he choked. "She's daid. She tuk de bullet dat would have hit me."

"No, Esau!" Nancy cried. "She's alive! She's not dead! She's still breathing. Where can we take her?"

They were led to Flannery's cabin where Esau laid his burden on a bunk. "Bring water and bandages," Nancy said. "Stay with me, Esau. You can help me. And you can help her."

Mike was not needed here. He mounted to the pilothouse. Flannery was there, handling the wheel, shouting orders to the deck crew and sending a succession of bell signals to the engine room.

The *Far Frontier* quivercd, then broke out of its inertia and came to life. Its power conquered the strength of the river, and the anchor line slackened. "To hell with the anchor," Flannery bellowed. "Use an ax on that line."

A blade parted the heavy line, and the packet was free. It gained momentum ponderously. The shoreline began to move past. Mike presently returned to the cabin. Nancy was still bent over the bunk on which the Indian girl lay. Esau was on his knees. Once more tears were streaming down his face, and once more he was praying that a life be spared.

Nancy looked up at Mike, her eyes big with a sudden joy that overcame all weariness. "She's going to make it," she said. "I feel it. I know it. The bullet made a clean wound."

"Thank thee, Lord!" Esau said, his great voice shaking. Nancy finished with the bandage she had been applying, and drew a sheet over Snow Dove. The Cheyenne girl was breathing with an effort, but she was breathing. It was evident the bullet had missed the lung.

The packet was now surging powerfully

ahead against the current under full throttle, and quivering from prow to stern. Mike placed a hand on Nancy's arm. "Stay off the deck," he said. "I don't want to lose you after all the trouble I've gone to so as to get you this far."

She still had the energy to make a little face at him. "Trouble?" she asked.

"That seems to be the word for you," he told her. "You've been nothing else to me."

He left and descended to the boiler deck. "How fast do you figure we're moving?" he asked the engineer, a bony man in greasy bib overalls.

"Faster'n we oughter be," was the reply. "An' we might be goin' a lot faster, but straight up instead of up the river, if'n thet boiler lets go. That crazy mick in the pilothouse ordered me to hang a chunk of iron on the safety valve. We've built up a bigger head o' steam than anybody in his right mind would ask a boiler to carry."

The *Far Frontier* seemed well supplied with fuel. The timber, cut to firebox length, was heavy and solid. "We tuk aboard all the *Far West* could spare when it left fer the fort," the engineer explained.

"Good!" Mike said. "We can use it. Fetch every spare man. Start piling more of it —"

"I don't take orders from nobody but the

cap'n," a stoker said. "An' not from a renegade thet looks like an Injun. An' I didn't sign up to fight Injuns. Thet's the yellalegs job."

Mike swung a fist and knocked the man sprawling. He waited for him to arise, ready to repeat the punch. The stoker, rat-eyed, weak-willed, did not get up.

"I'm giving the orders down here," Mike said. "On your feet, fellow, and get moving. Fast! And the same for the rest of you. There's no time to waste. You're going to be in the biggest trouble you've ever imagined before long. How about ammunition? How many guns do we have aboard?"

In addition to the weapons in the hands of the defenders, the *Far Frontier*'s reserve supply consisted of a dozen Springfields of the old-style single-shot models, and an equal number of cavalry pistols, along with a fair supply of shells.

"Load every rifle and short gun and have shells placed handy along the decks," Mike said. "Pile all this firewood along the rails, and see to it there are firing ports every dozen feet or so, wide enough to cover considerable territory."

A squad of cavalrymen had been left aboard the packet by Colonel Cool. They pitched in with the members of the crew to strengthen the barriers around the decks.

Mike swarmed over the boat, supervising the operation. "What's this all about, sir?" one of the troopers asked. "There's talk the outfit's in big trouble up the river."

He was a veteran soldier who had served under Mike in the past. Mike explained the predicament of the trapped troops and made no attempt to minimize their own danger. He realized he was taking a chance. The rivermen, in particular, would know better than the soldiers the odds against the packet's chances. He expected opposition, perhaps mutiny. These men were well aware of what their fate would be if the *Far Frontier* snagged and went aground on that west shore. There would be no escape for any of them.

One man decided to take his chances with the river, and leaped overboard at a time when the packet was within fifty yards of the east shore. He was the stoker Mike had knocked down. He had misjudged the savagery of the Missouri. He did not make it to shore. He was within a dozen strokes of safety when his head disappeared in a great whorl of water that boiled up around him. He did not reappear.

If any others had desertion in mind, that decided them against it. They reconciled themselves to the task of girding the flanks of the ship with the firewood.

Mike waited until the bulwark was placed to his satisfaction, then made sure all the loaded rifles and ammunition were in the proper place. "I'll tell when to open fire, and when to quit," he said. "Any man who doesn't heed will have to answer to me. When I give the order to open up I want every rifle to join in. There's nothing like massed fire to discourage the other fellow."

He mounted to the pilothouse. Flannery said grimly, "It won't be long now 'til we'll be dead fools or live heroes. Listen!"

Mike could now hear the same popcorn crackle of gunfire that had marked the battlefield from afar the previous day. "At least it shows we're in time," he said. "They're still holding out."

"Time fer what?" Flannery growled. He stared morosely at the shore. The channel that he had picked out had carried them within short pistol shot of the west bank. Mike could understand the captain's doubts. He was acquainted with Flannery's reputation. The man was one of those rare river experts who held both a captain's rank and was a member of that elite profession — the Missouri and Mississippi pilot's association. He was now showing why he belonged in that group. Mike felt that few pilots would have gotten the packet this far at top speed without meeting disaster. Flannery had done so by experience, instinct and nerve. All the familiar landmarks had been wiped out by the rising river. It was a different Missouri that Flannery was piloting. Past knowledge was of little use. Where there had been deep water a week previously there were now sandbars. Where there had been rock chains there was now water deep enough for a packet to ride safely through — provided the pilot had experience enough to judge the river.

The shore itself, as Flannery had said, was a fearsome thing along this stretch. It was girded by rapids and shallows and rock ledges over which the river boiled, white and wild.

"We'll need luck," Flannery said, wagging his head in the direction of the impossible shore.

The needle on the steam gauge stood firmly past the danger point. Flannery was still driving the packet at reckless speed. At times his beefy hand would reach for the bell to call for a safer pace. Each time he would look at Mike and his hand would fall away.

"Fools we are," he said. Then he grinned.

"McVey, you are either insane or you do not know that we could be blown to heaven on bits of boiler iron each minute."

The roar of gunfire came nearer with agonizing slowness despite the powerful drive of the paddles. The craft left a wake that was like the arched back of a prehistoric monster, extending back fifty yards from the stern.

"Down!" Mike yelled suddenly, his voice carrying to the decks below. "Down! Look out! Indians!"

Even as he spoke, the snake-tongue dart of gunflame came from the brushy, gloomy shore. Bullets shattered the upper windows in the pilothouse. Glass fell from the frames on the promenade deck. There was sibilant hissing and buzzing in the air. Arrows buried their heads in the log bulwarks and in the deckhousing.

A crewman reeled back, struck in the forehead by an arrow. The shaft had been sent with such force it tore through the man's brain, pitching him lifeless to the deck, his body contorting in the throes of violent end. His companions stared in horror.

"Stay down!" Mike yelled. "Keep your heads down! Hold your fire! You won't hit anything but air and trees. That's not the main bunch. Save your ammunition for the real fight."

Two or three crewmen did not heed, and began firing into the brush. Mike ran, crouching below the bulwarks, located the offenders, yanked them away from the ports and slammed them against the bulwark.

"Next time you waste shells I'll throw you overboard," he gritted. "Now reload those rifles and wait until I give the word."

He turned to find Nancy nearby. She had moved down the deck, keeping to cover of the barriers. "Are you sure your name wasn't Blackbeard in some other life?" she asked.

"You seem to be the kind that don't obey orders either," he said. "I recall telling you to stay off the deck."

She moved closer to him. Very close. "Are there any other orders, sir?" she asked.

Then she kissed him. Mike drew away. "What does that mean?" he asked.

She laughed at him. "What if I told you, Mr. Blackbeard, that I aim to marry you if we both live through this?"

Mike glared at her. "What about Marsh Prine?"

"What about him?"

"Now, let's not go into that," Mike snarled. "You were to be married to him."

"I wouldn't marry Marsh Prine if he was gold-plated and had rubies and diamonds for teeth. I never could understand why my cousin fell in love with him."

"Your cousin?"

Nancy's eyes were dancing. "Of course, you ninny. My cousin, Faith Armitage. She was the one who came west to marry Marsh. I only came along to be the maid of honor. I've been trying to explain this to you, but each time something else came up."

Mike kissed her. He kissed her again. And again.

"You deliberately let me hang and rattle," he said. "How long have you known I was on the wrong track? And I've spent a lot of time trying to figure out how to break the news to you that Marsh's broken heart mended in a hurry and that he's already married to the other girl."

Flannery's deep voice boomed from above. "Git ready! We're movin' in. We'll be in hell or back at Fort Flagg before this day is over, an' I'd say it likely will be the former place we'll end up in."

The *Far Frontier* had rounded a bend into view of the battlefield. Powdersmoke hazed the scene. The river had invaded the tongue of land.

The cavalrymen were still fighting. They

259

had drawn into a compact group on what evidently was the shallowest portion of their refuge. They had built a barricade of driftwood, which seemed to be in danger of floating away, and evidently had stopped at least one massed charge, for there were dead ponies and slain Indians in the shallow water near the barriers.

The tribes had now abandoned frontal attack, and, with the river as their ally, were waiting until their quarry would be forced to emerge into the open or drown.

The appearance of the steamboat brought a momentary halt to the firing on both sides. Then, great confusion swept the Indians. Swarms of warriors left the firing lines on foot and ran rearward. They soon reappeared, mounted, and began riding toward the river to join the original small party that had first discovered the approach of the packet.

Great numbers of warriors appeared on the shore, leaping from their ponies and taking to what cover they could find. Rifles opened up on the approaching packet — scores at first, then hundreds, as more Indians arrived.

The *Far Frontier*'s deckhouses were riddled, but the boilerplate and firewood took the sleet of metal and protected the defenders. Nancy crawled down the deck to the cabin where Snow Dove lay. Crewmen had piled wood high around its walls so that the major danger would be from a chance bullet.

Mike mounted to the pilothouse. He was exposed for a portion of the ascent, and bullets stormed around him, but he managed to dive into the protection of the wheelhouse with nothing more than a bullet burn on his shoulder.

Flannery crouched at the helm, peering through a slit in the armor. Mike moved to another slot. The packet was threading its way through drowned brush over flooded swampland toward the cavalrymen, whose position was still nearly half a mile away. Sizable trees jutted from the flood here and there. The prow of the craft crunched through a thicket of willows.

A rocky spine that would tear out the packet's hull appeared ahead. With massive strength, Flannery twirled the big, brass-trimmed wheel. The packet seemed to respond with agonizing clumsiness. Tensely, Mike waited for the impact. All he heard was a slight grating sound. The *Far Frontier* moved ahead, the rock chain sliding by on the port side.

Flannery bellowed a question, and the voice of a mate replied presently, "All right, so fur. Might have sprung a plank, but she ain't takin' any water to mention."

Indians mounted ponies to follow the steamboat's progress. They pushed the animals to their bellies into the river in order to come to arrow range.

This was what Mike had been awaiting. "Fire!" he shouted. "Teach them to stay clear."

The shoreward flank of the packet flamed with burned powder as every man opened up. Even the boiler crew crept to vantage points to join in. The Indians were driven to cover on shore, leaving some of their dead and wounded floating in the river.

Flannery uttered a grunt, and rang frantically for full astern. A giant, floating cottonwood that must have come from far up the Missouri had grounded in the brush, directly in the packet's path. Flannery continued to spin the wheel and play a tune on the engine bell. Mike again waited rigidly. The packet slowed to gentle headway. Its prow touched the floating tree at just the proper angle and the right point and swung it aside. It slid along the hull, bumping along, but doing no damage.

"Pretty," Mike said. "As a steamboat pilot, Flannery, I take off my hat to you."

Flannery did not answer. He rang for

more paddle ahead. He was a man entirely absorbed in his task. He was deaf and blind to everything else. A bullet shattered on the boilerplate. Particles of metal entered the slit from which he was peering and he flinched and reeled back. Blood streamed into his eyes.

He sleeved it away. "Take the wheel!" he barked at Mike. "Do only what I tell you."

The blood was from a gash on Flannery's forehead. The particles had missed his eyes. Mike leaped to the spokes of the helm while Flannery ripped a bandage from the sleeve of his shirt and tied it around his forehead. Then he returned to the slit and peered ahead.

"Port!" he snarled and yanked the cord of the engine bell. "Port, I tell ye! Don't ye understand English? The other way, ye jughead. Now, steady! Steady!"

Mike peered through the slit. Bullets and arrows beat against the boilerplate. The prow of the packet burst through another stand of willows. The battlefield loomed up less than a hundred yards away and directly ahead.

The defenders were desperately trying to cling to their barricade which seemed to be about to break up. The men were in water to their shoulders in many places, their arms, grasping carbines, above water, firing and reloading from ammunition boxes that were hung on the driftwood.

Mike saw Roscoe Cool. The colonel stood to his waist in water, his head exposed above a floating log. He was hatless, gaunt-faced, his graying hair plastered down his forehead. He stood here, not in defiance of the Indians, Mike believed, but in the hope they would kill him. This was Roscoe Cool's day of total disaster.

The *Far Frontier* lurched and reeled to starboard. She came abruptly to a halt. For a moment there was dead silence aboard. The men stopped firing, although bullets and arrows still tore into the bulwarks and deckhouses. Every person was waiting — waiting.

Flannery yanked the bell cord and Mike heard the gong sound below. "Full astern!" the captain was saying softly. "Full astern, old girl! Do this fer me. Fer the rigiment's sake. We're so close, so frightful close. We got to git 'em off. Only another boat length an' we'll be there. We're on a mud bank. Full astern, I say. Pull off!"

Mike heard the reversed paddlewheel churning. Muddy water boiled around the craft. For long moments that was all. Merely the roar of the paddles and the swirling water and the thud of bullets and arrows arriving from shore.

It went on and on until Mike could feel the dryness and the tautness grip his throat like fingers, until it became agony. He was thinking of Nancy, knowing what would happen to her if she was taken alive again. He was remembering that she had said she would not be taken alive. He knew that he must not let her hand be the one. It must be his own duty.

He saw great gouts of muscle standing out on Flannery's jaws. The steamboat captain continued to appeal to his packet, to its spirit, its strength. It was a paean of praise, an appeal, and a prayer. "Once more, darlin'! Once more, an' we're off. Now! Now! Fer the sake o' them poor soldier boys out there who are goin' to die unless we do this fer them."

Mike felt a tremor run through the decks. The *Far Frontier* moved slightly. Then she slid free.

"O'Brien!" Flannery bellowed in a voice that must have carried half a mile. "How about it below?"

"No damage, cap'n," the mate replied. " 'Twas mud we hung up on, not rocks. Hull seems sound."

Flannery took over the wheel and rang for

engine power ahead. The packet edged forward. She was now feeling her way over treacherous shallows. She glanced off some new obstruction, but survived.

Suddenly she was moving in deeper water upon the tongue of flooded land where the survivors of the regiment were cheering wildly, seeing their salvation.

Flannery rang for reverse wheel and the packet moved gently right among the embattled cavalrymen. They came swarming over the sides in a human flood. The rifles of the Indians took some toll, but the price was light. They brought with them their wounded and dead.

The last to be hauled aboard was Roscoe Cool. It was Esau Solomon who reached into the water, seized the colonel by the back of his belt and derricked him ignominiously over the rail to safety back of the barriers.

The *Far Frontier* began backing away, edging toward the main river. It was a feat of piloting as delicate as that of the arrival, but Flannery managed it, although the craft flirted with disaster on two occasions, but won free.

The last spent bullet from a tribal rifle flattened on the boilerplate and fell to the deck. Flannery cocked an eyebrow at Mike.

"If it's all right with you, McVey," he said, "I'll buy ye a drink in place o' the beatin' I promised. It has occurred to me that we look at many things the same way."

They shook hands. "I'll buy the second round and the third," Mike said. "I might even ask you to be best man at the wedding."

"Weddin' is it? Ah, yes, I saw you lolly-gaggin' down on the deck with the pretty redhead you fetched aboard. A fine time it was to pick for such things, what with bullets as thick as fleas around you."

Mike went below. Nancy was with Snow Dove. The Cheyenne girl's eyes were open. "She *will* make it," Nancy said.

Esau came to the cabin. "God answered my prayers, honey," he told Snow Dove. "You goin' to live. Everythin' goin' to be all right."

Nancy and Mike left them there and moved out on deck. Roscoe Cool saw Mike. The colonel had a bandaged arm in an improvised sling. He had lost a third of his command and knew that there never would be stars on his shoulders.

He started to approach Mike as though to offer an explanation, or even an apology. He thought better of it and turned away, still unable to unbend, even in the depths of his despair. Mike felt great pity for him.

Nancy swung Mike around, forcing him to face her. "Forget all that," she said. "Forget Colonel Cool. Forget the things that have happened. Above all, forget Marsh Prine. The important thing is that we're both alive, and all we've got ahead of us is life. I love you."

The steamboat, carrying its cargo of wounded and dead, but, above all, its living, was in mid-channel, traveling fast with the current toward Fort Flagg.

The flat where Esau's home had stood came abeam. From the nearby open door of the cabin they could hear Esau's voice. He was pointing out his place to Snow Dove. "Miss Nancy says she'll see to it dat I don' be punished fer what I done. Seems like her father is an important man back East, a 'Nited States senator, or somethin'. She say it's no good fer a man like me to live alone. She say dat some day you could help me live dar in peace, jest like me an' Ruth did 'til she went to de Great Spirit."

They heard Snow Dove's soft voice say something in Cheyenne. After that, they heard nothing.

Mike eyed Nancy critically. "So, I've been kissing the daughter of a United States senator. And a renegade like me has even got the brass to think she might marry me."

"Just try to get away," she said. "Do you think I'd let a man who owns three hundred pounds of gold slip through my fingers?"

Mike pointed toward shore. The draw in which he had cached the Black Hills gold was now a muddy torrent from rim to rim.

"I'm afraid I'm going to be a big disappointment to you," he said. "What if I told you there isn't any gold any longer? It's gone. The river has taken it. I'm afraid it's scattered down the Missouri from here to Council Bluffs."

Nancy peered at him wonderingly. "You're serious, aren't you? But you don't act like you'd just lost a fortune. I'd say you actually seem happy about it."

"That's the truth," Mike said. "It's a load off my conscience. I poached that gold in Indian country. I never could convince myself it belonged to me. It would have always haunted me."

Nancy kissed him. "You really are a renegade type, aren't you?" she said. "I'm looking forward to a lifetime with you. It's going to be a real joy. Who cares about a little, old bunch of gold? If you're happy, then I'm happy."

We hope you have enjoyed this Large Print book. Other Thorndike, Wheeler or Chivers Press Large Print books are available at your library or directly from the publishers.

For more information about current and upcoming titles, please call or write, without obligation, to:

Publisher
Thorndike Press
295 Kennedy Memorial Drive
Waterville, ME 04901
Tel. (800) 223-1244

Or visit our Web site at:
www.gale.com/thorndike
www.gale.com/wheeler

OR

Chivers Large Print
published by BBC Audiobooks Ltd
St James House, The Square
Lower Bristol Road
Bath BA2 3SB
England
Tel. +44(0) 800 136919
email: bbcaudiobooks@bbc.co.uk
www.bbcaudiobooks.co.uk

All our Large Print titles are designed for easy reading, and all our books are made to last.